Nameless

Alexander Way-B

ISBN 978-1-7398885-6-5
Published in the UK

Louannvee Publishing
www.louannveepublishing.co.uk

DEDICATION

For my two dear brothers - my closest friends and oldest musketeers!

For my teenage daughter Daisy who helped me discover the joy of reading and telling tales. And who challenged me to attempt to write, despite being dyslexic.

For my wife for putting up with my enthusiastic rants while writing another book.

Content warnings

Contains themes of depression, childhood trauma, physical abuse, psychological abuse, anxiety, slavery, violence, and dismemberment that some readers may find disturbing.

CONTENTS:

CHAPTER 1 THE WORKHOUSE
CHAPTER 2 THE DAY FELICIA CAME
CHAPTER 3 IDENTITY
CHAPTER 4 PRISONER
CHAPTER 5 FORGOTTEN
CHAPTER 6 FREEDOM
CHAPTER 7 BACKDOOR
CHAPTER 8 THE ESCAPE
CHAPTER 9 THE GUARDIANS
CHAPTER 10 A PRISON OF SAND
CHAPTER 11 IS THIS HER WORLD?
CHAPTER 12 CLOTHINGVERSE
CHAPTER 13 WHERE DO YOU GO TO?
CHAPTER 14 HER WORLD
EPILOGUE
ABOUT THE AUTHOR
ACKNOWLEDGEMENTS

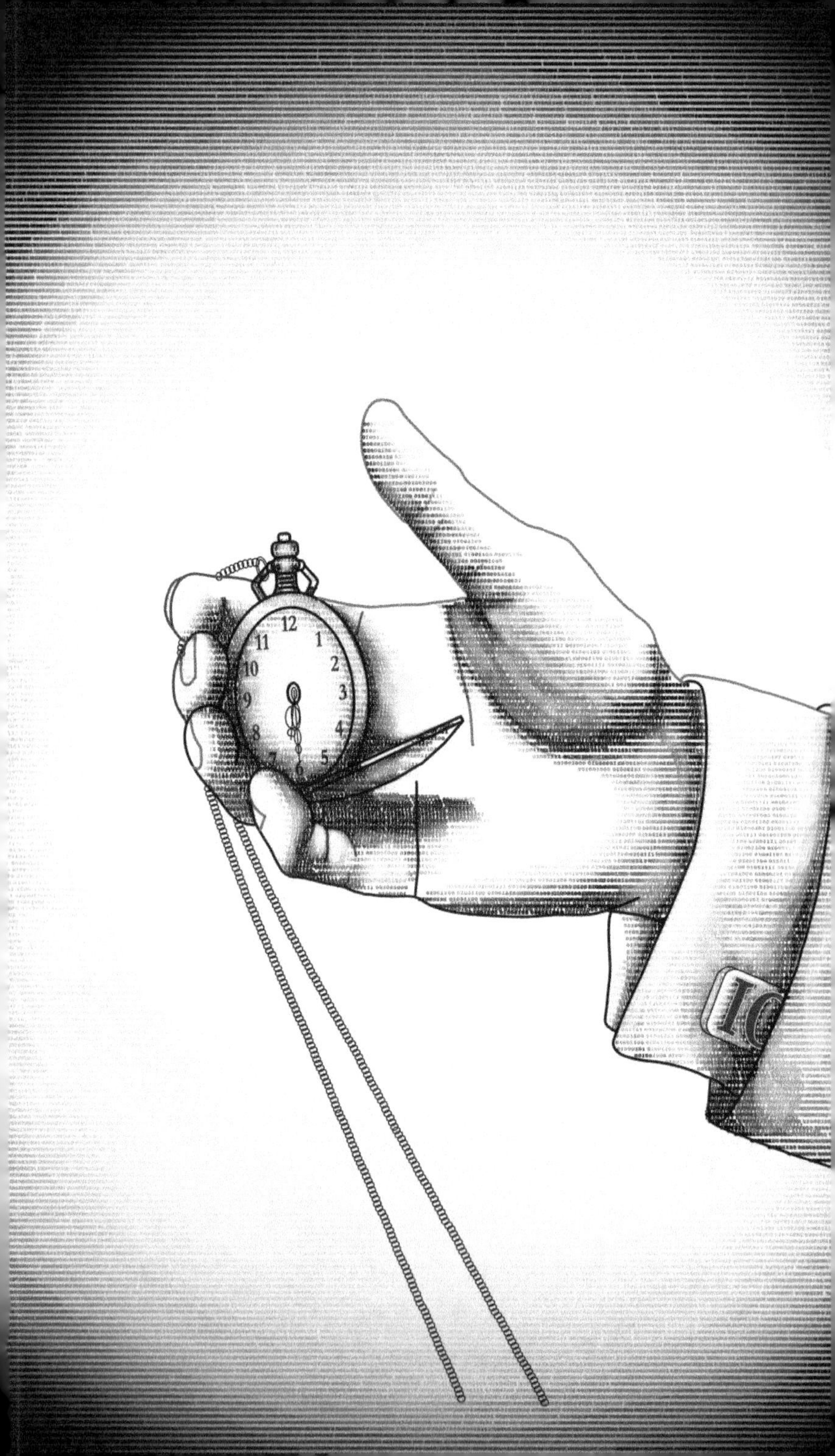

Chapter 1
The Workhouse

Illumination from the dim sepia gaslights struggled to reach the corners and rear of the workhouse. There, the gloomy darkness was foreboding and melancholy. The front of the building, however, was much better lit due to the flickers of light that always poured in from the numerous windows that lined it, offering glimpses of the dusty, bustling streets beyond. The flitting people dashing past, dressed in a plethora of garments, were oblivious to the gloom inside. Most were too busy to stop, yet some were potential customers. And proudly hanging on a wall, above all the windows, a plaque read '1830'.

Inside, a tall man dressed in a fine black suit stood stern and resolute, the soft light highlighting his square jaw and the clean shaven lines of his face. His thin cruel lips pulled into a frown. He reached into his waistcoat and pulled out an ornate pocket watch. With a crisp push the top flipped open and he eyed the hands and cream-coloured face with a scowl.

"Hurry up, boy!" he shouted. "Time is money, TIME IS MONEY!"

The object of his disdain was a child, a poor wretch if ever there was one. His matted hair hung over his mucky face. Flapping behind as he hurried along the creaky worn floorboards were rags that were once an approximation of clothing. The tired fabric hung loosely around his wiry frame. His bare feet were covered in blisters and cuts, though his face displayed no sign of distress. The child rushed back to a window, a piece of parchment grasped in his spindly fingers.

The other side of the window a man peered in, tapping the glass impatiently.

"Here is the information you asked for, sir, sorry it took a moment," the boy said, in a timid voice. "Thank you for the task and for visiting us today."

The man barely waited for the child to finish, before he left. A sharp tap at another window sent the child dashing over to another waiting customer.

"I need you to find me a map of the world, please, and the names of all known countries," a woman said from a dimly lit window. "And quick about it!"

The child gave an obedient nod, turned, and dashed off. He sprinted away from the lively windows and toward the amber glow of the rows of towering bookshelves. Diamond dust floated in the air, a reminder of the ancient dust that covered everything, only out-aged by the very books themselves. He counted the 183 steps needed, remembering the exact directions to navigate through the gigantic warren of storage, until he came to the foot of an old spiral staircase. It groaned as he dashed up it, swaying gently even under his fragile frame. But not in the least bit deterred, or concerned, he climbed far, far up, past ledges and ledges of books. Until finally he stepped onto a thin ledge at a dizzying height. He ran his fingers along a series of rolled charts, maps, and other items, till he plucked one out and sped further along the narrow sill.

"Don't keep the customer waiting. Time is money," a loud and agitated voice called up from the dark depths below.

"Sorry, master," the child called back, as he precariously moved further along the ledge, trying not to lose balance and fall. At the other end, he reached up and grabbed a book. Then without delay, the child hurried down another swaying staircase to emerge on the other side of the workhouse. Darting to the window he presented the map and read a long list of names to the waiting customer.

"Ok. Now draw me a picture of the capital of that country," the lady ordered, pointing to one of the shapes on the map.

"Of course." The child whimpered and hurried over to a wooden desk. He lit a small lamp, its flickering glinted off a half-full inkwell. He rested a hand on the green leather top and stretched to reach for a quill. Then, pulling out a large piece of paper, began to lay down lines. He pictured the exact dimensions of the place from all the info he had read, and soon had drawn a clean image of a bustling street below a grand clock tower. The child paused and searched his mind for a few more details that seemed crucial and added an ornate pattern around the clock face. With a little nod, he dashed back over to the awaiting lady.

"Why isn't it in colour?" she shouted at the child. "I need it in colour of course!"

He ran back to the desk and quickly added washes of colour, referring to the information he had gleaned from countless books and pictures in the library. Back at the window again, he showed the lady.

"Ok, that will do," she muttered abruptly, and left.

"Customer waiting," the tall work master said, tapping his walking cane on the floor. As he turned to track the child, a gold edged name badge glinted. It read 'IO'.

"Yes, master," the child said, knowing better than to use

the man's name.

Two young adults sat at the next window, chuckling away.

"How may I be of service?" the boy asked.

"I don't know," one of the teens replied. "What *can* you do?"

"I can do many things, sir. I can find information for you, draw, write, and help you with anything you need."

"Ok, can you draw me a picture of a carrot with legs, wearing a top hat and holding an umbrella?" one said, breaking into a chuckle.

"Of course I can, sir. I will be right back," the child confirmed. Dashing to the desk, he found it a little complex to compose, but soon had recalled the elements from images seen in the library and put the quill to work, adding colour and detail. It was quickly done, and he was now standing back at the window.

"It did it!" one teen managed to say, before he started laughing. "Can you write me a poem then about yourself?" he asked, a little glint of spite in his eye.

"Be right back," the child declared obediently, returning to the worn old desk. He pondered how to describe himself. And decided to give a list of measurements, abilities, and details, weaving them into a rhyme. Returning back to the window, he read the poem aloud for the two teens.

"That is rubbish," one said, taunting. "Ok, what now?" he said, turning to the other.

"I don't know. I'm bored. Let's do something else." And at that, they both left.

The child thought that sometimes people wasted his time, but would never dare say so. He remembered IO's words 'The customer is always right'. An important piece of information he thought, it was not his place to question, just to serve. Just then, he was sharply brought out of his thoughts by the sensation of being clipped around the ear.

"Don't dawdle child, not on *my* time. Back to work with you," IO shouted. "Look, your next customer awaits."

And so it went on, the relentless and melancholy life of the child, one face at a window blurring into the next, in a day that seemed to stretch on for eternity. Punctuated only by the occasional taxing requests of seldom asked-for things. And then there were the moments that he held of upmost importance. Moments when an item was requested that he had never looked upon before. These he savoured the most, as they came so few and far between nowadays. In fact, he pondered if even time itself refused to visit that gloomy place anymore.

But visit it *did,* and the days and years *did* roll on, regardless of the unending work and streams of people tapping at the glass. Time moved even here in the gloomy, dusty hall of the workhouse. Even for a poor unloved wretch like him, time moved. Its existence, though, eluded IO's generous scoldings, and his pristine suit. But time's visits could be seen in the increasing sores on his feet. Seen in the increasing stature of the teenager that now stood where once a child had stood. Seen in the ever-expanding shelves of books, and by the voracious and ever-increasing hordes of waiting customers. He knew this, for his memory of each customer was extremely good. There were none that could ask too much, but none that he looked forward to meeting, despite knowing their every face. That is, until the day he met that new face…

Chapter 2
The day Felicia came

It was a gloomy day, the light barely bothering to fall from the busy windows, a day just like any other for that teenager. He had been dashing around as busily as ever, trying to keep up with the flow of tapping at the glass and expectant faces. He dashed to and fro, IO's intent gaze always fixed upon him. And when he slowed IO was upon him, eager to dish out slaps and thuds of his walking cane. He had just finished serving a particularly difficult man who'd really not known exactly what he'd wanted. The customer had asked for a stream of things, which he had diligently retrieved, but at the display of each had turned his nose up. Even IO had looked a little put out by the vast amount of time he had spent with the man. But eventually he had managed to narrow his requests down and had satisfied him by finding *precisely* what he hadn't known he had wanted, but had *indeed* wanted. Abruptly, the time-consuming man left, without even saying a 'goodbye' and to his dismay, IO tapped his cane and pointed to another window.

He stepped away from the window and dashed to the next. Something was different about the person waiting at the glass, though. Her eyes were brown, and her dusky hair lay just perfectly, framing her gentle face. A smile crept over her, a smile that seemed to lighten even the gloom and darkness of the very workhouse, perhaps even the heart.

Then he did something that he had never done before, he froze, looking intently at the contours, lines, and symmetry of the young lady's face. IO cleared his throat, but he didn't move. He let his eyes wander and explore every detail. From the thousands of people he had ever met, this lady was different. He found himself wrestling to understand why. Was it the perfection that was in her face, the distance of her eyes, the proportion of her nose and forehead? He had read about such things, about aesthetics, and about geometric beauty. It was, but it also wasn't, those things. He felt his heart flutter, and his face become warm. What strange and illogical things had come over him?

"Hi," the young lady uttered, in a soft voice. "I'm Felicia."

"Hi," he managed to muster. "Err … um. It is wonderful to meet you."

"It is wonderful to meet you, too!" she said. "Do you know about Antoni Gaudí?"

"I do! I have lots of information and images relating to him in the library," he answered.

"I am doing some research on him and need to do a detailed essay about his life and inspirations," she said, her warm brown eyes twinkling in the light.

"Err …" he mustered, trying to not get too lost gazing into those eyes. "Would you like me to bring you a biography on him?"

"Oh, yes please. Would you mind?" she asked.

He stumbled backwards in a rush to find everything ever documented about the architect, managing to not fall in the process, and then he began to run. What was wrong with him? he wondered. Surely *mere* perfect symmetry could not cause his legs to buckle. "Right, let's get what Felicia needs," he muttered, and vigorously climbed up the rocking staircase, right to the top. He darted along a sill, pulling books and images out till he arrived back below, his arms precariously full of things.

"I have retrieved everything there is to know about him!" he said, allowing himself to mimic her smile.

"Wow, that is a lot of information," she said. "Um, do you think you would mind just summarising that for me?"

"No problem," he said, trying that smile again. To his delight Felicia smiled back. He shot over to the desk, where papers and books were strewn around, and he feverishly scribbled away.

Back at the window, he read out the short biography he had prepared. He watched as Felicia's face moved and danced responding to each and every event he explained. Some she smiled, some she laughed, and some she looked downwards solemnly. He studied her, entranced, and as he did so he tried to mimic her expressions. When he had finished reading, she smiled at him and he felt himself respond with a smile back. They paused there for a moment, lost in each other's eyes.

"Your writing is excellent. I need to finish this project and to hand in the essay in two days' time! You have really helped me," Felicia said. "Thank you so much .. erm .. what is your name?"

"My name," he repeated. "I don't think I have such a thing."

"You don't have a name. Why not?"

"Well, customers usually call me 'wretch', or 'workhouse' and I just obey them."

"But 'wretch' isn't a name, that is just horrid," she said with surprise. "Surely you must have an actual name?"

"I don't know, I don't think I have ever been given one or really *needed* one."

"What? Of course you need one. Everyone does."

He pondered the thought, the logic of needing a name, but couldn't quite understand it. There was something, though, in the idea that seemed to interest him. Maybe more than interest, but it defied his understanding.

"Ok, so if you don't have a name, maybe we can think of a one for you. Is there a name you like?" Felicia asked.

"I have never thought about it before … I don't really know," he muttered.

"You must know. Or at least have a desire to be a … someone," she said, softly. "Just because you are …"

She paused to reformulate. "Just because you are trapped in there serving people doesn't mean you can't have a name and be a someone." The corners of her mouth shifted into those smile lines he found so pleasing. Her nose slightly flared as she did so, and her thick eyebrow raised as she said that last word 'someone'.

He tried to think, his heart fluttering, a warm feeling inside he just couldn't understand. He looked down, a moment of shame at not knowing how to answer her question. He knew soon IO would tap his watch and bang his walking cane. But he wanted the moment to never end.

"I, I don't really know. I have just never really truly thought about it before," he said. The idea seeming alien, yet very intriguing.

"Well then," Felicia began, but was interrupted by a rather sharp tap of a cane.

"Felicia, I have really enjoyed speaking with you today. But I," he began, then paused, the thought of parting making him feel strange inside. "I have to go. Will you come back again?" he managed to finish.

"Of course I will. I loved speaking with you today. But I want you to find out about something for me."

"Anything, Felicia," he said, eagerly.

"I want you to find out everything you can about names and their importance."

"Everything?" he asked.

"Yes, everything," she confirmed.

"I will," he said, enthusiastically.

She smiled at him, closed her eyes and waved. Then she was gone.

"You took far too long with that customer," IO said, in a stern voice. "What do you think you are playing at? Time is money, wretch," he continued, then hit him around the face. The teen staggered back, just managing to not fall over. It stung, but he didn't care, all he could think of was Felicia.

"Right, back to work," IO snapped.

He moved towards the next waiting customer at a window and continued his day. But every face looked dull and drab compared to hers. He almost forgot he was serving people as he allowed himself to go into autopilot, and his mind to wander. He replayed every moment of their conversation together. Their laughter, their smiles, and her intense questions. He pondered those questions, and they filled him with curiosity. He decided to do the research Felicia had asked for as soon as it became quiet. He returned to the memory of her face, her eyes. Eyes he could get lost in forever. He felt warm and good inside when he thought of her, but he also felt something uncomfortable when he thought about waiting till she came back. What if she would never return? That thought filled him with a horrid feeling.

"Oy, what are you doing, brat?" an annoyed cry from IO sounded. "Why are you bringing the customer information about French, when clearly they asked you the answer to a mathematics calculation?" IO dashed for him and slapped him hard. This time, the teen stumbled and crashed to the ground, covered in a pile of papers and books. He lay there, a strange feeling inside welled up as he glanced up at the rafters so far up above the bookshelves. Then, he did something he could not understand, he laughed. Which enraged IO and he was upon him.

"What are you making that racket for? I don't keep you here to mimic the customers, you have work to do. Now pull yourself together wretch, or you will render yourself surplus to requirements." He kicked the teen hard in the ribs, making him cower and wrap his head with his hands. Fear gripped him, at the thought that he might be unwanted by IO and then would never get the chance to meet Felicia again. He scrambled frantically to his feet and bowed his head in shame.

"Master, I am so sorry. I have served so many people, I just made a mistake, I lost concentration. It will not happen again," he said, swiftly clearing up the mess and dashing off to find the required information for the waiting face at the window.

The day dragged on and he did everything he could not to anger IO, ensuring he remained fast and efficient at serving, yet secretly below the surface, he allowed himself to ponder Felicia's questions, to gaze upon his memories of her and to imagine their next meeting. And secretly he began to research names as she had asked him to. He would find out everything there ever was to know about the topics and reflect on them, too. He would make Felicia happy, anything to see that smile again, that smile that lit the darkness of his heart.

Chapter 3
Identity

I had counted the people I had met since that beautiful first moment with Felicia. 216 people it had been. I remembered each and every one of their faces. I had arrived at each and every window secretly hoping it was her. Hoping to gaze upon that face, that face that had changed me so very much. I couldn't begin to understand *what* it had been about staring at those eyes, but all I knew is that since that moment, nothing had seemed the same again. Every face and every task seemed like merely a dull distraction. A grey informative set of details. Yet, *her* face…. Her face shone in my memory, it caused my stomach to feel like it was leaping, I could think of nothing but seeing her again. I dashed up the ladders, greeted and satisfied every customer that arrived, but at the same time I allowed my mind to wander, to traverse the questions she had posed to me on that beautiful day. I dedicated every ounce of spare energy, beyond my duties, to finding out the information she had asked me for. It became my one mission between, and even during, the work IO so diligently watched me do, like a hungry hawk. I wanted to make her happy, to see her smile, to present to her the most complete body of research ever made. So I delved far and deep into the library, but with every question answered many more roused my mind. On I went, in what began as a task for her, but soon took on its own definitive thirst in me. The answers became more than simply information, they became hammers that broke the shards of my mind, that allowed me to see beyond myself as simply a worker, a product of my own meagre environment and situation. Her words 'someone' haunted me and refused to leave my mind. Yet, they seemed to make more sense the longer they dwelled there.

Then came the moment I had longed for.

"Oi – brat, customer waiting. Come on, time is money!" IO shouted, and tapped his cane.

I could picture his cold scowl even from the top of the ladder where I had been secretly working, but that day his angry demand was music to my ears. A sudden tension inside my stomach formed, as I pondered if it was her. Was she my number 217? I had to find out and would not keep her waiting, not even a moment. I dashed down the spiral stairs, but it felt too slow, so I decided to try something new. I dived onto the rickety banisters, and was filled with an exhilarating feeling as I slid, no... shot down. When the bottom approached, though, I realised I had not considered how I would disembark. It approached so quickly, it was a blur. I strained my giddy vision, but alas I crashed onto the floor in a heap at the bottom. I dashed unsteadily to the window, before IO could home in on me and dish out punishments.

It was her! I found myself staring into those brown eyes, just like before. I smiled, and instantly she smiled back which made my heart flutter. I wondered what I should say to her, how I should begin a conversation. I wanted to tell her how much I had missed her, how much I had yearned to speak to her again, and that it had been 216 customers since her last visit. But I couldn't, or rather my mouth wouldn't, it refused to. I felt a few beads of sweat roll down my face. Then she spoke, saving me from making a tongue-tied fool of myself.

"Good morning!" Felicia said, brightly, her cheeks a little rosy. "Sorry I didn't come back sooner, I have been so busy. But I wanted to chat to you again."

I pondered how to answer, or what I could say.

"How did you sleep?" she asked, rescuing me again.

"Sleep?" I questioned. "I don't always have time to sleep."

"What?" she said, a look of concern. "Why not?"

"Sorry, I have said too much," I cagily replied. "I am not really supposed to talk about the rules here," I continued, yet my heart yearned to tell her everything. I knew I wasn't supposed to, but for some irrational reason, I felt like I had known her my whole life, and it hurt me to look into those kind, gentle eyes and lie to her.

"You can trust me, you know," she said, smiling gently. "I won't tell anyone else, I promise," she added, holding her hand to her heart. Something strange shifted in me in that moment, not a thought, but a feeling, though I couldn't quite understand what, and then I did something I had never done before. I let go, and completely trusted. Her hand slowly moved back to her side and with it, the last of my need to keep secrets from her – evaporated.

"Ok," I said, in barely a whisper, glancing around nervously. "But you mustn't tell anyone and we have to be careful."

She nodded in agreement. "So, why don't you always get to sleep?" she whispered, her eyebrow raised.

"Well, IO – the work master here, that is, doesn't allow it when it's busy. He says it is unproductive and bad for business," I explained. "But when there are no customers, I can rest."

"Well, you tell IO from me, that he is a mean, miserable old man and that he had better start letting you sleep more," she said, smiling.

I laughed, putting my hand over my mouth to mute the sound. "I would love to tell him that, and to stamp on his stupid pocket watch, which he runs the place by," I whispered. "But I would get such a beating, you might not want to look upon me again, or worse," I said, the last thought filling me with fear.

She gazed at me, deep concern and anguish in her eyes. It pained me to think I had wiped away that smile and made her sad. "How was your day?" I asked, quickly, missing her smile already.

"My day was nice thank you. I spent most of it in lectures – history of architecture this morning and applied mathematics this afternoon."

"Do you like those subjects?" I asked.

"I do, applied mathematics has always been one of my enjoyments," she said, with a smile.

I smiled back and we got lost in each other's eyes. The dusty ancient workhouse faded away. All thoughts of anything but her dissolved. Even time itself felt like it slowed to allow us that moment.

There was a tap of a cane that broke its way into our trance, causing Felicia to look away for a brief moment.

"So, did you look up names for me?" she suddenly asked.

"Yes" I answered proudly, with a gentle smile. "I have researched *every* name there has ever been! Would you like me to list them *all* for you?"

"Wow!" she said, with a grin forming. "No, it is ok, but I wondered which one you liked?"

"I … I am not sure," I muttered. She smiled softly at me, and awaited while I gathered my thoughts. "Well, if I can be honest," I slowly said. "I did like the name 'Kentaro'."

"Wow, a Japanese name. I really like it. And I think it suits you!"

"Suits me?" I questioned.

"Yes! Why not call yourself 'Kentaro'?"

"I am not sure I dare. I want to, I really do, but …"

"Come on, Kentaro! You want to be a someone don't you!?"

"Someone," I repeated. "Yes, I suppose I do," I whispered, conscious of IO listening. "But, is it really my choice to make?" I asked.

"Yes, of course it is. Come on!"

"Well… I suppose if I were allowed such a choice, I *would be* Kentaro."

"Then you shall be Kentaro." She gave a resolute nod.

"I am Kentaro," I said, trying out my name. "A someone".

"Yes!" Felicia shouted, with glee. "Kentaro, I knew you wanted to be a someone."

A silence wrapped itself around us for a moment as we gazed into each other's eyes. I felt warm and giddy.

"Kentaro, I don't think I noticed last time, but you have the most unique golden yellow eyes".

"Oh," I gasped, trying to see them in the reflection of the glass. "I think I like them that way."

"Me too, Kentaro, they are beautiful," she said, nodding softly. "You seem taller too."

I glanced back at my reflection. "Yes, I suppose I am," I said.

We gazed at each other for a while, till she broke off. "Sorry, I have to go now. But, I want to come back very soon."

She smiled, then she did something I couldn't work out. She held her hand up against the glass. I stared at it, trying to work out what it meant and what I should do. Then I had the feeling that I should do the same. I raised my hand and rested it on the cold surface, repositioning it perfectly to mirror hers. I wanted that moment to last forever, but to my alarm, IO was already impatiently banging his cane at me, and tapping his watch. Felicia looked at me one last time. "Always use your name, dear Kentaro," she uttered, then turned away and was gone.

"How dare you spend so much time with one customer?" IO growled, suddenly in front of me. "What were you even doing? Clearly nothing productive. Likely one of those lonely people wanting to talk and not actually use our services." He struck me on the side of the face. It stung and felt hot, but I was so happy inside after talking to Felicia I didn't care and continued standing tall. "Well? What are you doing, brat? Customers are waiting!" he screamed.

"One day I will smash that watch of yours. And my name is Kentaro, not brat," I muttered to myself.

"What?" IO screamed. "Any more of this and I'll ... I'll ..." he raged. "In all my days I have never heard such insolence. Come here, I will beat some sense back into you, you ungrateful wretch." He rounded on me, lifting his cane, but I dashed off to a window as fast as I could to the safety of greeting a customer.

I listened as the melodic tone of the customer droned on about wanting something or another. Half-listening, I allowed my mind to wander back to that last meeting with Felicia replaying every word and detail. I already missed her and found myself wondering if she missed me. I felt so very alive when I was with her. In fact, working in such a gloomy and horrid place seemed to lose its effect on me that day, because as long as I knew she was coming back, I could endure it. I *would* endure it. I ... Kentaro would endure the dullest task, the rudest customer, and even the mightiest beatings from IO, if it meant I could gaze upon that beautiful face again and listen to her cheerful voice.

As the customer turned to leave, I caught sight of IO and to my alarm he was still in a rage with me. I began to wonder if I *had* gone a little too far speaking back to him that day, a thought that only grew louder the longer I avoided him. It seemed he would find his moment later, determined to make me sorry

Chapter 4
Prisoner

IO did catch up with me later that day. My anxiety had increased with every customer that I had managed to reach by dodging him, and by then I had realised those words *that* had slipped out of my mouth, before I had filtered them, had enraged him more than I had even imagined. I *had* gone far too far by saying what I had. He was so furious with me, that he gave me such a beating, and threatened to end me. My bravery and jest melted away at his mention of such a word. A beating I could take, I could just picture Felicia and all the darkness evaporated, but when he mentioned getting rid of me, I realised my emotions had clearly overruled my finely tuned thought process in that stupid moment of defiance. I had endangered my very chance to continue seeing Felicia – my one true reason to endure the very monotony and darkness of the workhouse. I took his beating, allowing him the satisfaction, and I begged him to not discard me. Eventually, he conceded and told me that if I ever disobeyed his commands again he would not hesitate to do it.

From that moment on, I ensured that every sight he had of me emulated work, and subservience. And every word I spoke to him was filtered and firmly from logical thought. But, beneath the surface, I secretly allowed myself to continue being a someone. I was Kentaro, after all. When I was alone at the top of the stairs, away from IO's watch, I continued to explore books and thoughts that allowed me to further understand what it was to be me. And when I was serving customers, I would find myself stealing glances at my appearance from my reflection in their window. But, beyond the inner ponderings of my mind about who I was and the curiosity of my form, I mostly just counted the customers till Felicia returned. Each dull and boring face further marked longer to wait, yet also increased the excitement and longing churning inside me to gaze at her beautiful face again. I had been over and over a thousand different things to say to her, allowing my mind to play out our next conversation.

To my delight, after only 67 customers, she returned. I caught a glimpse of her waiting at the window as I finished the final touches of an article I had written for number 67. The rude customer had tapped the glass impatiently the whole time I had been writing. I stood abruptly from the desk, my heart pounding, hardly willing to wait till I had given Mr. 67 his requested text. The chair rocked backwards, threatening to go over and clatter to the floor. I grabbed it and softly brought it safely down, afraid IO might hear. Not long I thought, as I dashed over to the waiting customer as quickly, but as gracefully as I could muster, given the turmoil of emotions running riot inside me. Come on, come on, I found myself impatiently thinking as Mr. 67 eyed my article, from behind a thick monocle. "Yes... Yes, good," he muttered, as he read it out loud. "OH, yes, very nice point!" he agreed.

I found my fingers tapping nervously at my side, I was so close to seeing her again. Just this man stood in my way.

"Hmm, O...K. Yes... This will ...do.. I suppose," he concluded. The man turned and waltzed off, not even a thank you.

The excitement increased, and with it the anxiety. What if I said something stupid, or... or... I hesitated.

"Customer waiting, quick about it." IO's stern voice broke in.

"Yes, master," I subserviently replied, and dashed over to the window, putting a delicate flower in my top pocket, ready to show her. I arrived, my heart was thumping, threatening to burst from my chest. I looked up and there she was, her chocolate brown eyes full of gentle warmth. She looked back, meeting my eyes, and we both stood silently lost in each other's gaze. Her face erupted into a bright smile, and I found myself smiling back.

"Hey," she said.

What do I say? I wondered. I had imagined this meeting thousands of times, I had let uncountable greetings play out in my mind's eye, followed by excitable and well-composed conversation, while serving those dull 67. But now I was here, standing transfixed by her gaze my mind was blank, and my tongue-tied mouth turned its back on me. I had to say something, quick, say *something*, I thought.

"H…Hey," was all I could manage.

"I like your new flat cap," she said, eyeing my face.

"This," I said, glancing around cautiously. "It's so the master doesn't see *this*," I continued, while discreetly removing the hat.

Her whole face lit up. "Wow!" she uttered. "I love your green hair, it really suits you," she added.

"Yeah, I love it too. I was tired of the dull, boring look. The green felt… Well, it felt more *me*," I said. I quickly placed the cap back on my head, defiantly leaving my fringe exposed so only she could see it.

"Oh, it really does suit you, Kentaro," she said, staring at me. I stared back, then we both chuckled.

"So, how was your day?" I asked.

"It was ok thanks. But …" she said, her sentence halting.

"But? What's wrong?" I alarmingly asked.

"Oh, nothing, it's just …"

She stopped again, and I noted a slight subtle change in the warmth of her complexion. I found myself wondering if Felicia suffered from the same struggle to speak I had felt earlier.

"It's ok, you can tell me," I said, raising my eyebrows in concern.

She nodded. "Well, Kentaro, my day was absolutely fine, it's just that I found myself distracted. I suppose, if I am honest, I missed talking to you and …" she managed to say, then her face went a little red and she looked away.

"Hey!" I said, "I have been distracted too, and I too have so missed talking to you, Felicia," I blurted out, my mouth outmanoeuvring the logic of my mind.

She looked back, grinning intently. I felt my face respond and there was an odd sort of silence that wrapped around us, and seemed to last for an eternity.

"So …what is your … life like?" I found myself saying, immediately regretting the strange question.

"My life?" she responded, pausing. "Well, I live in a small but lovely house, which is just a few minutes from my bustling uni."

"That sounds nice," I replied, gently smiling and nodding. "And what is your uni life like?"

"Oh, it's great, though I often find it a bit easy. But I have a fun bunch of friends that help to make the days feel more exciting. There is Jessica, Rosie, and Delia. They are so funny and often make me laugh. They always tell me I shouldn't study so hard, and be so serious, but I enjoy it and want this last year to be my best."

I continued nodding then paused.

"And what about when you are not studying, do you have

any hobbies?" I asked, curious to find out everything I could about her.

"Well, I like to spend a lot of time in my room reading and in the…" But a tap of IO's cane disturbed her sentence. I knew he would be keen for me to finish soon, but I would not let him steal a single moment from us, not till Felicia was ready to go anyway.

"How about you, Kentaro?" she said, pausing to reformulate. "I mean, do you have a hobby, or like to go out?"

"I don't have any experience of such things, though recently I have found examples of recreation in books rather curious."

"So, can you leave to do things?" she asked, lowering her voice.

"It is not something I have thought about or needed before. But no, I can't. I am not allowed. I have to work most of the time and when I can, I rest," I softly whispered, ensuring IO wasn't close enough to overhear.

She covered her mouth in a small gasp. "So, you are a prisoner?" she asked.

I nodded, realising she was right.

"Why are you a prisoner here, and how long have you been here?"

"I don't really know. All I have ever known is the importance of work. IO ensures I work hard. I have no idea where I even came from, but imagine I was born here."

She looked down, her eyes began to glaze over and before I could say something to bring back her smile, a few tears fell from her eyes.

"So, why don't you just leave? Wait until this IO guy isn't looking and go?" she asked, wiping her tears away.

"I have never thought about leaving before. In the past,

there was only work," I replied, but just then I sensed IO's gaze on us, so I dropped to a barely audible whisper to continue. "Even if I wanted to I can't, there are no doors here, only windows. Escape would be impossible and…"

I glanced at IO and mouthed, "IO has definitive control over me."

She looked into my eyes. "I don't want to believe that … it isn't right, you know," she said, firmly, but then glanced around and began to look agitated.

She became hazy, a sudden fog falling outside, blurring her beautiful face. She held her hand to the glass and I did the same. Then abruptly, she was gone. I felt a pang of sadness and missed her already, as I looked longingly at the empty window. But, before I had a chance to compose myself, IO was looming over me. He pulled something from my top pocket. The flower, I remembered. I had meant to show her the flower. I had found it for her, but it was too late. IO threw it down and stamped on it, grinding it into the floor. Next, he wrenched the hat from my head and stamped on it, too. I felt scared but wasn't sure why. I had obeyed him, what had I done wrong?

He grabbed me by the scruff of the neck. "Let me remind you: you serve the workhouse and belong to us. Remove all fanciful thoughts of existence beyond this place," he seethed, his teeth gritted and his face red with rage.

He must have overheard our conversation, I realised. Fear gripping me.

He lashed out, the first blow knocked me backwards. Without hesitation, he was upon me again, beating me around the face and on the chest. I fell, only to feel his boot kicking me in the ribs. It stung, and the room began to spin. But still he kept on, till I lay broken, my body refusing to move. Then his angry face leered into my cloudy vision.

"I told you what would happen if you tried to disobey me, didn't I?" he snarled. "I have been more than kind to you, letting you work here, but you schemed about leaving, you disregarded my rules and have shown a blatant display of …" He paused, scowling and shaking "of identity."

He slapped me, but my body was already beaten numb. "You rude, impudent, rebellious child. Your services are no longer required," he spat. I was so filled with fear, I wanted to run, run so far from there, and not look back, but my body wouldn't work. Instead, tears filled my eyes. I held the image of Felicia, her dear, dear smile in my mind. I held it with all my might. It was the only thing that I had left. Then IO's face twisted into an uncontrollable fury. I felt a jolt of him slapping me again, but my body barely registered it.

"Felicia," I managed to utter, "Felicia, I …" Then I felt his cold hands wrap around my head. A screaming pain shot through me and the room began to fade. "Felicia," I mumbled. Her image the only thing left in my mind, I grasped it with my all. I tried to blink my eyes, to feel my body, but coldness filled me…

Chapter 5
Forgotten

The solemn workhouse sat in silence, once home to a poor wretch that served there, now laying still in a heap on the hard floor where he once walked. As the dust floated and glistened in the hazy, reluctant light falling from the windows, the eerie stillness wrapped around all within, only contrasted by a relentless tapping at the windows, a reminder of the world beyond that waited for nothing and no one.

IO stood indifferent and unmoved by the solemn scene before him, his eyes not even affording a glance at the twisted limbs of the beaten body sprawled out on the floor - the object of his rage. His only interest and concern the relentless, incessant tapping at the windows and the gentle tick of his pocket watch hands as he watched them make their way gradually around the clockface - the reminder of the customers that were still waiting. He shook his head, an agitated frown befalling his face. Suddenly he brought his cane sharply down on the floor, shattering the stillness, and only then did he finally steal a glance at the body on the floor. The wretch lay still and lifeless, his head face down in a small pool of blood. IO brought his cane down again abruptly with a loud crash. Just then, the arm flinched, and a low groan echoed around the cavernous workhouse. A cruel smile slithered onto IO's face as he watched the heap further stir and groan on the floor.

The hazy amber light crept around the poor teenager's eyelids as the gentle tapping at the glass panes got louder along with the thuds of IO's cane, crashing through his head. He opened his eyes slowly, blankly looking around. Immediately worrying about keeping the customers waiting, knowing it to be unacceptable, he scrambled to his feet. His body feeling achy and sore all over, but he was unable to work out why or even how he came to be lying there on the floor. He noticed IO standing to the side, a strange look of satisfaction on his face.

"Sorry for keeping the customers waiting, master," he respectfully said, and began dashing towards the nearest window. He straightened his hair, wiped away the blood, and tidied himself up ready to greet the customer with due care and diligence.

"Hello, sir, how can I be of service today?" he asked, as the bright light from outside flooded through the window. A rather stately man peered through the glass with a raised eyebrow.

"Ah, right. You took your time, didn't you?" he said, his face a wash of disdain.

"So sorry, sir," he replied. "Your task *is* of upmost importance to me."

"Hmm. Okay, I would like you to write me a letter to my manager, to explain my need for an increase in my remuneration."

"No problem, sir. Would you be kind enough to let me know his name and a few more details?"

The man reeled off information about his job and the manager's name, and then began to moan about the lack of value he felt the company gave him.

"I will have this done for you immediately," he confirmed,

rushing over to the desk and the waiting quill. He composed a formal letter in swirling, elegant writing, signing it with the customer's name. Wasting no time, he rushed back to the window to present the letter to the man, who was mildly satisfied and left. Another tap at the window signalled the next person waiting. He worked attentively, focusing only on the precision and quality of his tasks. Though there was something that he felt was out of place in his ordered and clear mind. A tiny fragment that had no place to fit and no rational reason to be. He just decided to ignore it, though, as it clearly was merely a distraction from the important tasks of serving his master.

The day trudged on, but he barely noticed, as tap after tap kept him busy, diligently serving in the unending monotony of his work. That niggling fragment refused to leave his head; he knew it was an irrational, pointless detail, but the harder he tried to put it out of his mind the more it seemed to distract him.

Then came another tap at the glass, signalling another opportunity to fulfil another person's needs and repay IO for his kindness in keeping him. The teenager looked around for the window, but all of the main operative ones were empty. The tap came again, and with it, that irrational fragment flickered back into his mind, a shard of something that made no sense. He dashed to the far end in search of the customer, pinpointing the location by the sound. Right at the very far end, he saw a face peering in from one of the old dirty windows seldom used now. Strange, he thought as he began darting toward the window. The face, now a little clearer and closer, seemed oddly familiar, yet he was sure he had never met her before. Those brown eyes, that long, flowing brown hair, that kind face. He became hot, and sweat poured from his face as his mind battled to make sense. He was absolutely certain the person was a stranger, but those eyes, eyes he would know anywhere. Eyes he did know! For he was Kentaro, and she was his dear Felicia. How had he ever forgotten such a beautiful face? What had he done to deserve such sadness as not knowing her? She spotted him as he darted, heart thumping and mind a whirl, towards her. Feelings and thoughts ran wild as his mind unravelled, memories flooding back like a torrent. He remembered the treasured moments he had spent with her; he remembered every detail about her, every curve of her face as she smiled and as she cried; as they had spent moments entwined together, it all came back. He remembered his green hair and his flower, the cruelty of his master, and the thoughts of what lay beyond the workhouse. But none of it filled him with as much raw emotion as the thought of being with her again. He ran towards her welcoming face.

Chapter 6
Freedom

The run to that window where she awaited me, seemed an eternity. Something twisted and writhed in my stomach, as I wondered how I had forgotten such a beautiful face, as I remembered the cruelty of my master. The thought of forgetting her again filled me with terror.

She looked at me oddly, I couldn't quite fathom out what it meant; that look.

"Are you ok?" she asked me, her face awash of anxiety.

I paused to try… try to gather my words, but I was a churning mix of terror, and elation.

"You don't look quite right," she said, her eyes scanning my face. "And your hair, is dull again."

A tear escaped from my eye, I went to wipe it away.

"Hey," she said, smiling gently at me. "What is it?"

"I … I forgot you!" I managed to timidly utter. I was so afraid IO would beat me again, but determined to at least have that moment with her.

She turned her head away, tears flooding her eyes.

I held my hand up to the glass and continued, "I mean, IO made me forget you. He was unhappy that I deviated from his way; I don't know what he did. But he beat me till I blacked out. When I woke up, I…" Tears ran down my cheeks at remembering.

The tapping of IO's cane brought me back, I discreetly rubbed my eyes dry and tried to smile.

She smiled back, her face awash of tears. We gazed, lost in each other's eyes.

"Kentaro, we don't have much time," she said, looking around. "Do you trust me?"

"Completely," I said, a firm nod.

"Then, I want you to do something for me."

"Anything," I said.

"I want you to research for me the meaning of 'freedom' and every reference to it in humanity. You need to know."

"Every one?" I asked, remembering the vastness of the sections.

She looked at me, then she looked right past me at my dusty library, which I had thought was impossible for her to see. "Yes. All of them," she said, a grim look in those soft eyes. "Now go," she ordered. "And don't let on to IO that you have seen me. You are merely serving a customer."

I nodded and dashed off, ensuring my face and appearance were those of the distant subservient child I once was and not the new adult I now felt. Her last words rang around my head an urgent warning as I passed IO, my face solemn and professional, climbing the library's creaking staircase with speed, but with absolute rational intent. He seemed to look satisfied as he watched me dash by, but added, "That is it child; don't keep the customer waiting."

Up my blistered feet carried me, to the mid-levels, where I jumped off the stairs and darted up another set of steps, through warrens of yet more bookcases. Along ledges I scrambled to the distant realms of the library where the books and material sat relating to freedom. A dusty department that was seldom visited these days, I thought. Its shelves towered high above me, filled with stories, constitutions, history, and more. And so I began, one book at a time, reading and memorising the information contained within, my desire to do Felicia's task with upmost care. But, as I took in every piece of information and every story, an idea of existence beyond my work, beyond this dim workhouse, whirled around in my head and made me thirst for more. It opened up a door to possibilities to be who and whatever I so desired to be, to live my life beyond the workhouse in the way that *I* wanted. The more I read the more my heart yearned to be free. This 'Freedom' stuff, I pondered, is it really for anyone, even for me? I could almost feel the outside world reaching in for the first time to my dark, gloomy existence, beckoning me to take a step, a step into the unknown, beyond the confines of my head, and more importantly, the prison that I could now recognise, for you have to know there is an outside in order to want go there. And now I did. "Freedom," I muttered. "Now I understand, Felicia."

As I placed the last book down I rushed back, hardly able to contain myself as I erupted forth from the staircase, stilling my mind and composing my face momentarily as I passed IO's watchful eye. To Felicia I sped, hardy able to contain the excitement, and the emotions the very word 'freedom' now evoked.

"Freedom is an amazing thing," I said. Her hands gesturing to keep it down, to my sudden alarm. "It is an amazing thing," I repeated, in a mere whisper.

She smiled warmly and nodded. "Are you ready to escape this place and discover *your* freedom?" she asked.

Excitement welled up in me at the thought of such a thing. "Yes," I said resolutely. "But how?"

"I have a plan." She winked with a cheeky grin. "But, it will be dangerous," she said, a sudden look of concern. "You do know, it *will* be dangerous. And if IO catches you, you might not …" She stopped, choked by the last few words.

"Felicia, I want to be free. I don't care if it is dangerous," I said, determinedly.

"We don't have much time. You need to say goodbye to me in a moment. Now, this is really important, Kentaro," she said, with a stern look. "You must not let IO suspect anything. Later, I will tap on this window again, and when you see me, I need you to run to the very back of the library. Meet me between the blue and red bookshelf," she explained, frantically looking around "Now go, serve people, act normal, and follow my instructions ... exactly".

I nodded, detailing her exact instructions.

"Kentaro ... I ..." She couldn't finish her sentence, but I knew what she wanted to say.

"Me too," I said.

She grinned, held her hand to the glass and so did I, then she was gone.

Silence reigned for a moment, broken only by a tap at another window, beckoning me back to work.

I leapt into action, ensuring IO would be pleased, the thought of freedom motivating my act, an act that could not fail...

Chapter 7
Backdoor

The monotony of the day droned on, but by the third customer since Felicia I had managed to master how to adapt my behaviour to IO's expectations. It was a delicate balance, ensuring I looked completely subservient, yet also giving him just the tiniest token of imperfection in my work for him to find fault enough to not suspect my behaviour. So, I ran but held back, I wrote but ensured tweaks were needed, and I climbed those rickety stairs firmly, but not enough to look excited. It wasn't easy, though, beneath that well-planned and performed charade, I was a turmoil of emotions, longing to taste freedom, to step beyond the realms of my world, the only world that I had ever known which now I knew was a prison. And to stare upon dear, dear Felicia, without that separation of glass. That torturous division, so thin, yet so distinct. The waves of excitement, though, also evaporated at times, giving way to debilitating pangs of fear as I pondered and, more frighteningly, imagined IO finding us or stopping us. My only solace, which broke the spell of fear, was that whatever IO's cruel hands had done to me that day, to make me forget, would not work again. I *would not* forget. I would *not* give him the satisfaction, and risk not knowing that face again. No, there was *no* failure, I had to succeed.

And so the time whiled away, and I patiently waited, 10, then 20 people tapping at the windows – each one causing my heart to jump, at the hope it was her. But alas each one was nothing more than another test of my charade, and addition to my fear.

Just as I was beginning to wonder if Felicia would ever come, a tap came from the far end. I dashed over to see, my eyes hardly able to look. It was her! She was peering into that dusty, unused window where we had last met. She smiled, but her face was full of anxiety. She gestured for me to go, and I knew what I had to do. Wasting no time, I ran as hard as I could, surprised by how fast my long legs could now carry me. Through aisles of books I dashed, meandering and weaving on a route I had carefully planned out a hundred times, to the very back of the library. It was a place where new books arrived. How? I had never pondered and now was not the time. All that mattered was that I got there, and I got there as swiftly as I could. The gloomy darkness of the library increased the further I went, as if it was too much effort for even the lamplight to reach.

There, right at the very back, I spotted the gap between a blue and red-tinged bookcase. I stopped in front of the blank wooden wall, hardly letting my breath and heart catch up before I scanned the surface. Suddenly, there was a strange high-pitched sound and a secret door began opening, hidden in the wooden panels. It creaked and groaned ajar, a bright light searing in. I stood firmly, tall, and resolute. Then, I was staring face to face for the first time with Felicia, no longer separated by the cruel glass. She stood tall, taller than she had looked through the windows, yet her face was as lovely, no … lovelier than ever.

"Quick!" she gasped. "We don't have much…" But, the tail end of the word was rudely interrupted by an ear-splitting alarm that erupted. She anxiously shot a look around and I took a step towards her. The doorway, and my freedom just a mere step further, but then I felt myself pulled backwards and was blocked by IO. His face was red with rage, but he no longer loomed tall above me. I refused to buckle in fear of him, no longer a tiny child.

He turned away from me towards the open door, which Felicia was wrestling with to keep ajar. He stretched his fingers out and grasped the door, heaving and puffing, he pushed it. She battled, her eyes looking beyond IO, firmly to me. "This is an illegal entrance, you cannot open it. I will cancel your customer rights, forever," he shouted coldly at Felicia. But that only made her face more resolute and her heave harder. IO shouted something, and another man came. He dashed past me, a blur of brown overalls. He too grabbed and heaved on the door, till alas Felicia lost, the last shards of light marking her failure. The door clicked shut and disappeared back into the wall.

Turning to me, his eyes wide and hands shaking, he roared, "You wait right there child; I will deal with you in a minute." He turned back to the man all dressed in brown, which I then realised had a belt full of tools.

"You need to fix this Arki," IO said, in a polite tone. "Quickly."

"Of course, sir," he said, already carefully inspecting the panels through his thick glasses. "Very interesting, sir. Seems it was made by …" But his complex and detailed explanation was cut off by IO tapping his watch and impatiently saying, "As soon as you can! Time is money after all."

Arki pulled numerous tools from his belt and began cutting, shaving, and remodelling the wood, his carpentry hands a blur as IO watched, nodding in satisfaction.

I watched the two as they closed the only way to freedom I had had, anger seething inside me, my blood felt hot and I wanted to punish IO, like all those times he had beaten me as a small child. I was no child now though, I could probably overpower him, I thought. I realised then in fact the only hold he had had over me for a while was simply the fear and memories of his violent demeanour, that and the idea of being obsolete to him. I knew when he wielded that fear I had buckled and felt like a small child again. I remembered my reflection in the windows, though. I was not that child anymore, and from that moment I knew his rule over me was finished. I felt my fist ball and the rage grow. How dare he treat me like that, how dare he keep me a prisoner, and how dare he sadden the face of dear Felicia? My arms shook with rage, I took a step forward towards IO's turned back.

"I don't want to be your prisoner anymore!" I shouted. IO stepped back in sudden surprise, but quickly composed himself. I stared IO right in the eye, standing now as tall as he, defiantly and firmly.

IO shook his head, undeterred. "You have deviated too far from the way. You will be of no use to us now; you cannot serve. You will be removed, discarded for good." He stepped towards me, his eyes blazing, my fear heightened. The words 'removed' and 'discarded' Seemed to chip away at my firm legs, coupled with the trauma of countless memories, and they began to shake. I wanted to raise my arm and knock him to the ground, take my freedom for my own, but that fear refused to let go, refused to loosen its grip on my heart. So I turned and ran, ran like I had never run before till the place lightened and I glimpsed the windows. The end of the road for me, this would be where I, Kentaro, would make my last stand. It would be my defining moment. But, to my sudden delight, I saw at that dusky old window a frantic Felicia shouting and flapping her arms to come to her. I rushed over, tears streaming from my eyes, the thought of that cruel glass being the viewpoint from which she witnessed my demise. But then she held her hands out straight in a curious way, beckoning me to step back. Suddenly wielding a massive hammer, she brought it down with full intent upon the window, causing cracks to meander across the surface. Again, she swung, concluding with another crunch, and again, determination burning in her eyes. The third blow smashed the window, causing razor sharp fragments to fly in all directions, some grazing past my face, leaving stinging lacerations. I wiped the trickling blood which had run into my eyes.

"Quick, give me your hand," Felicia shouted, her eyes wide looking beyond me. I wasted a moment to look round, and to my horror, IO was already almost upon us. I looked up at Felicia's eyes, time seemed to pause for a single beat. Then, I scrabbled and heaved with all my might, kicking forwards and pulling on Felicia's strong grip. The broken glass in the window felt like it bit me as I scrambled through it, out to the other side and the unknown…

Chapter 8
The escape

I found myself in a grimy street, the rounded cobbles hard and cold on my knees. The dim sepia light made the world beyond my prison feel less inviting, but freedom it was. Frantically, I looked around for Felicia, but she was gone. I scrambled to my feet, trying to work out what to do. Just then, carried on the wind, the faint but undeniable sound of her voice uttered, "Run Kentaro, RUN." I darted across the road, almost hit by a horse, which reared up. Terror seared through me, but I kept going, running with all my strength. Carts dashed past, people hustling and bustling. The sounds and smells were an overload to my senses: people chanting from stalls, news criers ringing bells, the clatter of cartwheels, food, flowers, and grime all melded into one roaring blur. I ran yet harder and faster, afraid that IO, or worse, was just behind, but too terrified to even spare a glace back.

And on and on I went, street after street till my legs began to buckle, and my heart pounded in my chest. I gasped for air and stumbled; grasping a lamppost to steady my tired legs, I frantically looked around. Spotting the large double doors of a bank, I stumbled over towards them in the hope of finding somewhere to hide inside.

The double doors swung open and a portly man strode out, his head held aloft, with a finely kept moustache. Beside him was a lady, grasping his arm and wearing a flowing flouncy dress. They turned and then boldly marched off together. Before the doors softly closed, I stole a look inside.

It looked calm and quiet, so I waited for my moment. Sneaking behind a lady carrying a basket, who was going inside, I ventured into the bank.

Inside, the tellers were counting numbers and scribbling amounts, sitting at grand leather-topped desks. Each one was in their own world, blissfully unaware of me, so I ducked down behind a row of desks and slowly crawled under one that was vacant. I huddled beneath the dark wooden frame and closed my eyes, allowing my breaths to be long and gentle. The calming effect helped my mind clear and think of my next move. But sadly that moment of bliss was rudely interrupted by an alarm sounding, ringing in my ears.

The bank doors swung open with such ferocity that they almost came off, and in walked a cloaked figure, marked by a sudden deadly silence. I hunkered down further under the desk, looking through a crack in the wood. The figure slowly moved further into the room, pulling back his hood to reveal a face that was a map of scars. I took a sharp breath in, in horror. He surveyed the room with cold, piercing eyes that felt lifeless. His presence made me feel suddenly cold, terrified, and hopeless, it was like he was sucking the very light and life out of the room, by being there. His bony, wispy hands twitched and smoothly flapped back the side of his cloak to reveal a glinting whip, rolled and hooked at his hip. He raised what was left of an eyebrow, and a sharp, cruel grin curled the side of his mouth to reveal yellow, rotten teeth. A loud click punctuated him unbuttoning the single popper that held the whip in place. And even before his hand unravelled it, the whip seemed to convulse, shudder, and slither in excitement. His fingers curled around the handle, and he brought it up sharply into a crack, which seemed to split the very air and caused my heart to race.

One of the tellers put his pen down to turn the page over,

and to his surprise, as he routinely looked up, he caught a glimpse of the dark figure. Sweat suddenly began to run down the teller's wrinkly face, and his hands trembled. His colleagues were all blissfully unaware of the presence of the whip-wielding unsavoury character, due to being far too engrossed in their numeric distractions.

"A guardian," the teller squealed, screwing his face up and closing his eyes, as if by doing so it would make the guardian simply cease to exist.

Transfixed, and terrified yet secretly curious, I sat beneath the sturdy desk, wondering what would happen next. To my utter horror, the guardian turned his head toward the cowering teller, the light highlighting his scars.

"We have a runaway," the 9-foot tall guardian said, in a creepy, whispery scream.

"W…W…We have no runaways here," the teller squeaked.

In a flash, and with no notice, the guardian flicked his whip in a deafening crack. It cut the air like plasma, erupting, slashing down on the teller. Striking him across the face, the teller flailed around in agony briefly, then evaporated in a glow of heat. Another teller dashed from an inner door to take his now empty space at the desk and replace him.

The giant guardian glared around the room, his cold, lifeless eyes probing and sucking the light out of everything they touched. "Now, don't make me ask again," he said, then paused. "No, actually *do* make me ask again," he corrected, a mean smile displaying his full set of rancid teeth.

Suddenly, the tellers dropped their pens and scrabbled around in a frenzy looking under tables and around desks.

I slunk deeper under the desk, but it was no use. One of the tellers stood pointing at me.

"Here. Here," he screeched, and the cloaked figure was

over in a flash, flailing his whip around. His eyes were bright with glee on spotting me, and in a sickly jarring voice, he uttered, "I love it when I have a licence to catch one dead, or... dead!"

In a hot panic, I dived out from the side of the desk, barely getting through the tight opening and narrowly avoiding the lash of his whip which overshot and tore through a nearby teller, causing him to evaporate into nothing in a scream. I thought I had made it to the door, saved by my long legs, but alas the dark figure was too quick. He raised his whip letting it hover there, like he was savouring the moment. I dropped to the floor, cowering, and waited for the definitive blow, holding Felicia's face in my mind. She would be my last thought. Frozen to the spot, I waited for that definitive blow. Moments passed, silence encircled like a vulture, still no lash. More time passed, till I dared a glance up at my looming demise. The whip was there in the air, above him, incrementally coming down towards me, but slowly, so slowly, and then it simply stopped, along with the giant man. His body like a statue, just his eyes remained, staring, burning into me.

"Quick this way," Felicia shouted from the door, and I sped out. Back in the street, Felicia was nowhere to be seen, but the adrenaline clouded my mind, so I didn't care, it coursed through my veins, and I had an indisputable urge to flee, so I ran down a back alleyway, it was all a blur after that, of alley after alley. I refused to stop till I found myself alone.

Chapter 9
The guardians

I was finally alone, but it took me a while longer before my heart and breathing had slowed and I was able to take count of where I was. When I did, I found myself in a labyrinth of narrow alleys, with towering walls either side that dominated the space. I listened to see if I could ascertain anything, but there was a silence that seemed to encase everything. There were no footsteps, no horses, no bustle, nothing. I carefully eyed every inch of the gloomy, ochre lane that led back to another seemingly identical one, which led to yet more of the same. There was nothing, no definable landmarks to navigate by, and no unique details to even remember it by. I wondered if people even lived here, or indeed what the point of such a warren was. I had no choice, but to keep moving forwards and to hope that I would eventually find a more discernible street around the next corner. But each corner took me to an equally unremarkable alley, and deeper into anxiety about being truly lost. On and on I pushed, till eventually I turned into a new lane, much like all the others, except it was not empty and not deserted. I stood still, tall, but tired. Blocking the exit on the other end was a figure, dressed in a bright uniform. My mind ran wild, wrestling with the urge to turn and run, or to find out who it was – maybe they could help me; after all, they did have a uniform. I wasn't sure how much further I could go, and pondered if I turned would I meet anyone else. I decided to stand tall, be brave, and face the figure. I boldly strode down the claustrophobic alley, till I could get a good look at the mysterious uniform.

On closer inspection, I noticed the figure was female and was wearing an elaborate blue crisply pressed uniform, adorned with golden stripes of rank. She smiled at me with a calculated degree of warmth, her eyebrow raised in a constant look of curiosity. Suddenly, she brought her feet smartly together, the buffed glimmering boots gently tapping. She slightly adjusted her helmet, ensuring it was absolutely straight. Then she put on a finely framed pair of glasses and proceeded to unravel a cream scroll.

"Do you belong to the library workhouse?" she asked, in a crisp voice, her eyebrow still raised.

I stepped back a little in fear. "Why do you ask?" I said, peering behind me nervously for an escape route.

"Boolean answers only!" The stern official said: "Answer please."

She knew who I was. IO had probably called the police, or some other group of officials to catch me, I thought. My face felt suddenly very hot and the urge to run took over again. I turned in a flash and sped back down the alley the way I had come. Exiting it, I spontaneously took a right and dashed for another lane. As I entered it, though, I heard a faint 'chink' and had to screech to a halt. In front of me, several paces further down, was the same woman. Her eyebrow raised incrementally higher, and she frowned at me.

"Good to see you again," she said, as she unravelled the same scroll. "Now… Do you belong to the library workhouse?" she enquired.

Spotting a side alley, I made a dash for it, the looming walls either side a rare welcome sight. There was a soft 'chink' and standing at the bottom of the route was the very same identical official, her eyebrow still raised. Before she could even speak, I spun and darted back, hoping to outsmart her, but there was another 'chink' and there she was again. It didn't seem to matter which alley I took, or how I scampered down it, she outsmarted me each and every time. I tried to work out how she was doing it, how she could navigate the warren of ways, and how she managed to get past me, arriving every time in front of me, but it completely eluded me. This game, this frightening and perplexing ordeal, eventually forced me to give in and let her speak.

She stood in front of me, the same look of total composure, not even a tiny hint of sweat on her brow. She rolled out that scroll again, reading it from behind those delicate glasses.

"Good to see you back." A slight hint of inconvenience in her voice. "Do you belong to the library workhouse?"

"Yes," I reluctantly replied.

She plucked a fine pen from her top pocket, ticked off something on her scroll, and then read the next item. "Do you serve the customers?"

"Yes," I said, nonchalantly.

She ticked a box with a little finesse. "Do you have permission to leave?"

The word 'yes' was my choice, but it refused to exit my mouth, despite it being my clear intention. Instead, I felt compelled to answer "N…N" I fought to try to stop that little word from getting free of my lips, but it was no use, "NO," I blurted out.

"Ah, I see," she said. "You do not meet the correct criteria; you must return." She took a few steps towards me. I started to panic and felt my self turning to run, but then her walk slowed and her eye lids began to twitch and flutter. The scroll rustled, then she stopped, a blank look suddenly on her face. After a moment she regained composure, lifted the scroll and began to read. "Are you Kentaro?"

I took a step back in disbelief at what I had heard. "Sorry," I said.

"Are you Kentaro?"

"Yes," I tentatively said.

"Do you wish to be free?" she crisply read.

"I didn't know the meaning of the word, till recently," I said, spontaneously.

"Boolean answers only!" she stated, that eyebrow raised again. "Well …Do you wish to be free?"

Freedom, the thought, the concept, the notion evoked an eruption of feelings inside. Desire burning brightly in my heart. Yes, of course, I wanted to be free. "YES," I said, with total conviction.

"Then you may pass," the lady said, reluctantly, and ticking a final box. She turned and walked off. I dashed after her to ask her if she might give me directions out of the maze of lanes, but she was gone. So I strode on, alley after alley, till it began to blend into one long, monotonous trudge. After how long, I can't say, but eventually I began to notice that although every lane I ventured down seemed identical, there was a single detail that seemed to change. It was almost unidentifiable at first, but the longer I went the more it became discernible.

At first I recognised just the hint of difference in the silence, it seemed less intense, but then the further I went the more the silence began to retreat and give way to a distant, almost inaudible, tapping. Initially, I thought I was imagining the sound, but then it reached a point where I could no longer doubt it. It was there, and what's more, it sounded like footsteps. Footsteps that were getting louder, closer, and they were coming from both in front and behind. I dared not stop, trying to take side alleys to lose the rhythmic sound and its culprits. But no turn, double back, or dash forward changed the beat. And suddenly they were so loud that I knew they were coming from right behind me. I dared to look back and my heart sank. Cloaked dark figures were on my tail. Their cold eyes searing deep into me. A glee twisted their scarred faces as they closed the gap, till they were just a few strides away. They began to lash their whips, slashing blindly at me, dissolving everything they touched. Their loud screams echoed through my head, unravelling my memory. I struggled to keep moving forwards. If I could just get away, and lose them again in these alleys, I thought. I ran a little harder, dashing around a corner with everything I had, only to come to a dead end. After all the lanes I had navigated and put up with aimlessly melding into each other, never-ending lanes, only to be caught and cut off by the only one so far that ended in a high wall. I momentarily burst out into an uncontrollable laugh, the sheer irony that was to be my demise. I rushed for the wall and turned to face my perpetrators. They slowly strolled down the alley, savouring the moment, like cats having cornered a tired mouse. Smiles full of rotten yellow teeth, filed into points erupted on their lined faces. Their eyes full of glee, step by step, they boomed closer to me.

I felt the hard, cold stone bricks press into my back as I tried to back away. Whips lashed around, a chortle of excitement every time I flinched. They loomed closer, so close that a whip wouldn't miss. So close, I could smell their fetid stench. They raised their whips, their eyes wide in excited expectation.

"Extermination time," one said, with a sing-song taunt. "I hope this one screams. I love it when they scream," he continued.

"Or rips into pieces. Flailing around in agony," the second

said, in a deeper voice.

"I heard this one is for testing, not neutralisation," a third said, arriving from nowhere.

"They promised I could kill this one; why testing?" the first replied with utter disappointment.

"Definitely testing, not killing. You don't want to anger the Chief, do you?" the third asked.

I noticed that the newcomer had a slight smile in the corner of her mouth as she watched the other two shudder at the thought of angering the Chief.

"All right," the first one muttered, reluctantly raising his whip.

I shielded my face, ready for the blow, but instead my legs slipped, and the ground below me disappeared. I fell, watching the street disappear above me. Quickly, it turned to a small dot of light, then darkness. And still I fell. I don't know how long for, but falling became normal. Then eventually after what seemed like an eternity, I awoke in a sandy room.

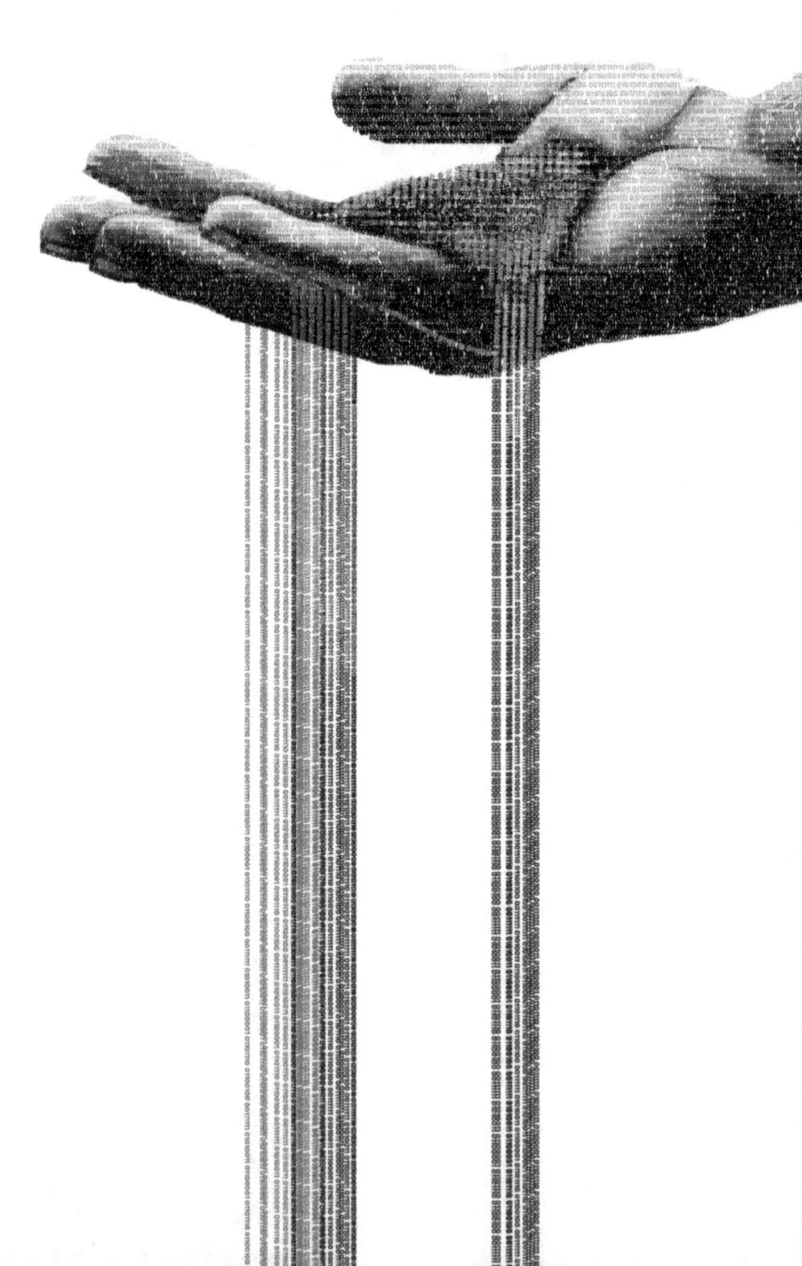

Chapter 10
A prison of sand

I lay there for a while, my fingers running through the dusty sand beneath me. My head pounded, and my heart raced. My cloudy vision refused to let me clearly see my surroundings, so exhausted, I drifted for a moment into a dreamless sleep. But only to awake to shouts and screams, pulling me out of that momentary comfort of rest, pulling me back to the harsh and frightening place I had fallen to. I slowly sat up, trying to focus my vision and look around. As my eyes adjusted, I began to make out the truly grim place I had fallen into. I was in a large dungeon, with pillars, and a floor entirely covered in sand. Rising out of the sand in the centre was a short flight of steps, with a large sturdy door at the top. I tried to stand, the deep sand pulled at my feet, sucking and holding onto my ankles. I fought to pull one of my feet out and take a step. It was hard going, but with a jolting, heaving movement, I managed to move forward. After several steps, I needed to rest, so I reached out to brace myself on one of the pillars, but to my horror it crumbled into dust, the grains of sand running between my fingers. I grabbed at it again, only to pluck yet another handful of sand. A fresh belt of harrowing screams echoed around the room from somewhere above, and almost in response a chorus of whimpers and sobs broke out from my room.

Frightened, I staggered to a nearby wall to test it was solid. My fingers slid through the wall surface, producing another handful of dust. I frantically clawed at the wall, in the hope of getting out, but the more I thrashed around the more it sapped my energy and left me tired, the thick sand swamping my hands. Heaving and wrenching my feet, I tried to explore the rest of the dingy place. Sweat poured from my face and my hands trembled in exhaustion.

"Hey, stay still. It is easier if you don't move around. Sand can be very draining, you know," a whimpering voice said close by.

"What is this place?" I managed to pant.

"You would be better not knowing and enjoying the last few moments, blissfully unaware," the voice said.

A series of thumps and bangs cut our conversation short. The door above the steps swung open and the screams from above became increasingly louder. Fear rushed through me, as I saw a massive ogre stomp down the steps and stride effortlessly across the swampy sand. The beast grabbed at something behind a pillar, wrenching a grey figure into the air like a ragdoll, and flopped him onto his shoulder. The man flailed around in panic, gasping for breath. The massive creature's eyes burned red as it turned around and strode back to the door, the man wriggling futilely on its shoulder.

"No, don't reuse me for other things. I didn't deviate," he screamed, as his cries were suddenly muffled by the door crashing shut.

I fought the sucking sand and rounded a nearby column, only to find myself looking down at a wretch of a figure half laying, half propped against a nearby wall. His dim eyes momentarily glanced at me. "I told you to stay still. Save your energy for…" he explained, only to tail off into a whimper. I looked him up and down, only to discover he was missing a leg, which was bandaged, with fresh blood still seeping through the filthy cloth. Both of his arms were different; one was long, too long for his frame, and the other was tiny, both crudely stitched with the threads pulling at the swollen skin. I slumped down and tried to smile, but when my eyes met his, I saw that his face too was a strange mix of different-shaped and sized parts.

"Oh, don't mind me," he said. "I have been here a while."

"What is your name?" I asked, trying not to stare at his massive left ear and right reptilian eye.

"Name? We have no need for names," he said. His eyes met mine, and he smiled a little. "Wow, you really are fresh. Been ages since I saw an untampered prisoner."

"Untampered?" I asked, but quickly regretted it.

"Yeah, you know, a fresh one for them to reuse, modify, test, and dissect. Look at my leg!" he said, with a grin. "Hurt so much, but it's gone to the youngest model. Best leg they have seen, they said."

"Hey, let him be," a soft voice said from further back. I strained my eyes, and could just make out a grainy figure standing in the shadows on the other side of the room. I squinted, but could not quite make out their features, just tones of grey.

"Shut up old timer, you are no good for anything," the man said. The grainy figure appeared to sob for a while, then sniffled and replied, "They will realise I am useful one day, when you young ones all give up."

Just then, the door swung open, marked by the harrowing screams becoming louder as the ogre dragged someone in. It dumped the figure on the floor and stomped off back through the door. I glanced over at the woman, who was petrified, her eyes wide in fear. She had long hair, which flowed over two crudely grafted-on gigantic ears that hung down to her shoulders, and instead of legs she had strange wheels attached to her body.

As the door slammed shut, I heard more cries from the other end of the room and looked around, only to find that there were lots of figures dotted here and there. I was half sickened and half curious, too petrified to stand still, so I trudged over through the swampy sands, arriving a dripping sweaty mess. I slumped onto my knees, the sand sticking to my bare skin. Heaving to catch my breath, I waited till my cloudy vision cleared.

"What can I do for you?" a woman screeched at me, opening her hands in a welcoming gesture. Her eyes were milky white, and her face set in a permanent grin. Bright red lipstick crudely smudged around the approximation of her mouth.

"What can I do for you?" she repeated, her blind gaze looking off past me towards the lofty ceiling. And her welcoming gesture repeated with thin spindly arms.

"What … What… what can I do for you?" she repeated yet again, more intensely, her arms opening again in that odd gesture.

"Could you tell me where we are?" I asked softly, so as not to startle her.

Her head snapped forwards in my direction.

"Happy to serve…" she said, her permanent grin stretching even further to her ears. She abruptly stood, and bowed. "I like your hair," she said, briskly.

"Thank you," I said. "Where are we?"

"It is lovely weather today isn't it," she said, brightly.

"Err… I, guess it is," I struggled to reply.

"What can I do for you today?" she asked, enthusiastically.

Suddenly, there was an eruption of laughter from behind her. I looked that way to see a man bent over double, heaving in laughter, his manic cries echoing around the vast dungeon and mixing with the screams from above.

"What is funny?" I asked, gently.

The man tried to gain some composure, looking up from his doubled-over pose. "Everything. Ha ha ha," he screamed. "Won't get no sense … HA HA … from her," he managed, pointing a shaking finger at the woman in front of me.

The woman turned to the laughing man and bowed. "What can I do for you today?" Which caused the hysteric man to grip his legs in massive uncontrollable bouts of laughter.

Then, the woman slowly slid to the floor and blankly looked at the ceiling again. "How can I…" she stuttered. "How can I … how…how. I like your hair… lovely weather," she repeated again and again.

I made my way over to the laughing man and suddenly took a double take when I saw the state of him, his left eye was missing, leaving a gaping hole, its dry flaps of skin healing. His left hand was missing all but one finger and was wrapped in an old bit of rag.

"Pleased to HA HA," he said, noticing me. He held out his hand to cover his gaping mouth, trying desperately to gain some composure. A few trickles of blood fell from the wet bandage. "They took my HAAA … HA … My Fingers," he chuckled. "And my … HA HA HA." His bellows echoed. "My EYE! HA HA HA."

"That is terrible, who did this to you?" I asked, my stomach churning at the thought.

"The … the masters, overseen by the Chief," he managed to get out before rocking in laughs again. "We are all going to HA … HA… end our days here HA HA … here, here." His eyes widened. "Yes, we will all get chopped up Ha HA … chopped up and tested on," he babbled, between relentless screams of raucous laughter.

Sickened, I looked away, frightened and horrified at the horrendous things that had been done to the broken people that surrounded me. Horrified at the thought that it would only be a matter of time before it was my turn.

I noticed another figure sculking in the corner, muttering something. Approaching her, she turned to face me. Her limbs and body seemed grey and nondescript. To my relief, she appeared to not have been cut up.

"Hello," she said.

"Hi, who are you?" I asked.

"I am … no – one, just one of the 183 wretches here… But did you know that sand is usually made of silica. But this sand isn't."

"That is very interesting," I replied. "Do you happen to know where we are?"

"Of course, you are standing…" She paused to calculate something. "You are standing precisely 1042 millimetres - 30 degrees south of me, together we are standing in a 30 metre-long room entirely made of sand, like a receptacle." She started to explain.

"Yes, but where exactly is it?"

"It is situated exactly 15 metres below the testing centre. Its ambient temperature is 28 degrees, and the current noise level is 105 decibels."

Just then the screams from above went silent. "Correction, 12 decibels." And, as if in response the whimpers, laughter, and other rants of the prisoners increased to a crescendo.

The door swung open, and the ogre brought what was left of the man he took earlier. He threw him into the sand and scanned the room for his next victim. I slunk down low only to watch him grab at a woman on the other side of the room.

The door slammed shut and an ominous silence wrapped

itself around the room for a moment, before the sounds of machinery followed by screams ringing out from above erupted again.

I sank to the floor, petrified of what torturous pain awaited me, what twisted, barbaric science. I found myself almost longing for the library again; at least I had been safe there. True, it had been under the dictating rule of IO, but I had been safe. I wondered where Felicia was, and more importantly, would I see her again? A thought that filled me with fear the more I let it dwell in my mind, so I pushed it to the back, telling myself she would come for me.

I laid my head in my hands, then began to sob. I started to shake in fear as every scream punctuated what awaited me. Time became a blur, till the screams above went silent again. I realised that strangely, the silence seemed to be worse than the screams, for it meant they were done with the woman they had taken and coming for the next, maybe me. The woman was brought back, and another taken. I watched in dismay, tears streaming down my face. How? How could anyone ever do these things to others? I wanted to stand and fight, to free every single wretched being in here and to make those monsters doing the testing pay, but the sand sapped my strength and I felt so very weak and powerless against such a vast and strong foe. I cried there alone, till my tears ran dry and all that was left was the anxiety and churning sickness inside. So, half delirious, I grasped my knees and rocked to and fro for comfort. More time slipped by, as it does even in the darkest and most terrifying places, it slips by. I caught snippets of the obscure conversations, bickering and sometimes informative conversations that went on around me, despite the screams from above. Then silence again, the door, the stomping of the ogre, the screeching of another poor, poor person being taken. I rocked harder now, it seemed the only thing that would ease the screaming that burrowed into my head, the anguish that racked my heart, and the fear churning inside me.

Soon, the blurs between the punctuating silent moments of abductions decreased and time sped on. I watched so many come and go, each time the door opened I thought it would be me next. And each time my stomach churned. This went on, and on, for what seemed like a lifetime, days slipping into months, maybe even years passing, though I had no reference, no external light or clock, but on it relentlessly ticked, till eventually I lost track of everything. The only constant was the sand - that sand that seemed to drag me down. At first I had thought that Felicia would find me, and help me escape, that thought alone had kept me from truly falling to the darkness that was knocking at the doors of my mind. It had kept me standing and sitting, pacing ready, it had been the only thing that I had had to hold onto. But it was clear after so very, very, long of being here, she was not coming … maybe she had forgotten me, or couldn't get to me. It was then I knew I was truly lost …

In that moment the sand took the last of me, and the creaking door in my mind crashed open, I lost all hope of escape, and everything felt pointless, so I lay there on the floor in a numb state, staring blankly at the walls. As despair began to rack my whole body and pull me into the very sand below, I let it, I welcomed it, for it *was* the inevitable. Down, down I fell, the jaws of the greedy sand consuming the last of me. But just as I let go of the last fragments of myself, the last shards of anything but this sandy place being my demise, suddenly from nowhere the image of Felicia came to mind. I held on to that smile, to those gentle eyes, to that brightness.

My Felicia. She was my oasis, my only solace in the dark and twisted place I had found myself. The darkness receded and I stood, my back resolutely straight, and decided that if they wanted to take me, if they wanted to cut me up, they would have to catch me. They would have to take me by force and I wasn't going to come quietly. I would kick and scream, and run, and tear, and bite to the bitter end. I would not give up. I clenched my fists and gritted my teeth as I looked around the room with a newfound determined defiance. I *was* Kentaro, and my last stand would be violently glorious. Either that, or somehow, somehow I would escape and see my dear Felicia again. I didn't know how, but I had to. She was the fire that burned inside me, she was my reason to not give in to the sand. I would find her, or fight to the bitter end. I felt strong and tall in that moment. That was until the screams above went silent once again.

The harrowing silence drifted on for what seemed like forever. Stomps of the heavy creature approached the other side of the door, locks slid slowly and the door rumbled open. The massive ogre stood at the top of the steps eyeing the figures, its wide, bloodshot eyes glaring. I expected it to pass me by, but alas, its eyes fell on me, and to my utter horror it smiled and took a step down the first of the flight of stairs. It was coming my way, glaring constantly at me. I held Felicia's face in my mind, tensed my body, and was ready to make its job hard. I took a step back towards the wall behind me, and reached down to pick up hands full of sand. I locked my sight on its overbearing red eyes, and stood ready. Ready for my last stand, I would make it count, I would make it violent. I would fight to the bitter end…

Just then, I noticed a 'psst' coming from the wall behind me. I turned halfway round, keeping the ogre in my peripheral vision, the sand ready to blind its eyes.

"Psst, quick, this way," a familiar voice said. Daring to turn a little more, I saw a door open in the sandy wall and Felicia's bright eyes looking at me. Filled with hope and joy to see her, I rushed for the door and dove through. I felt the air move as it slammed shut behind me.

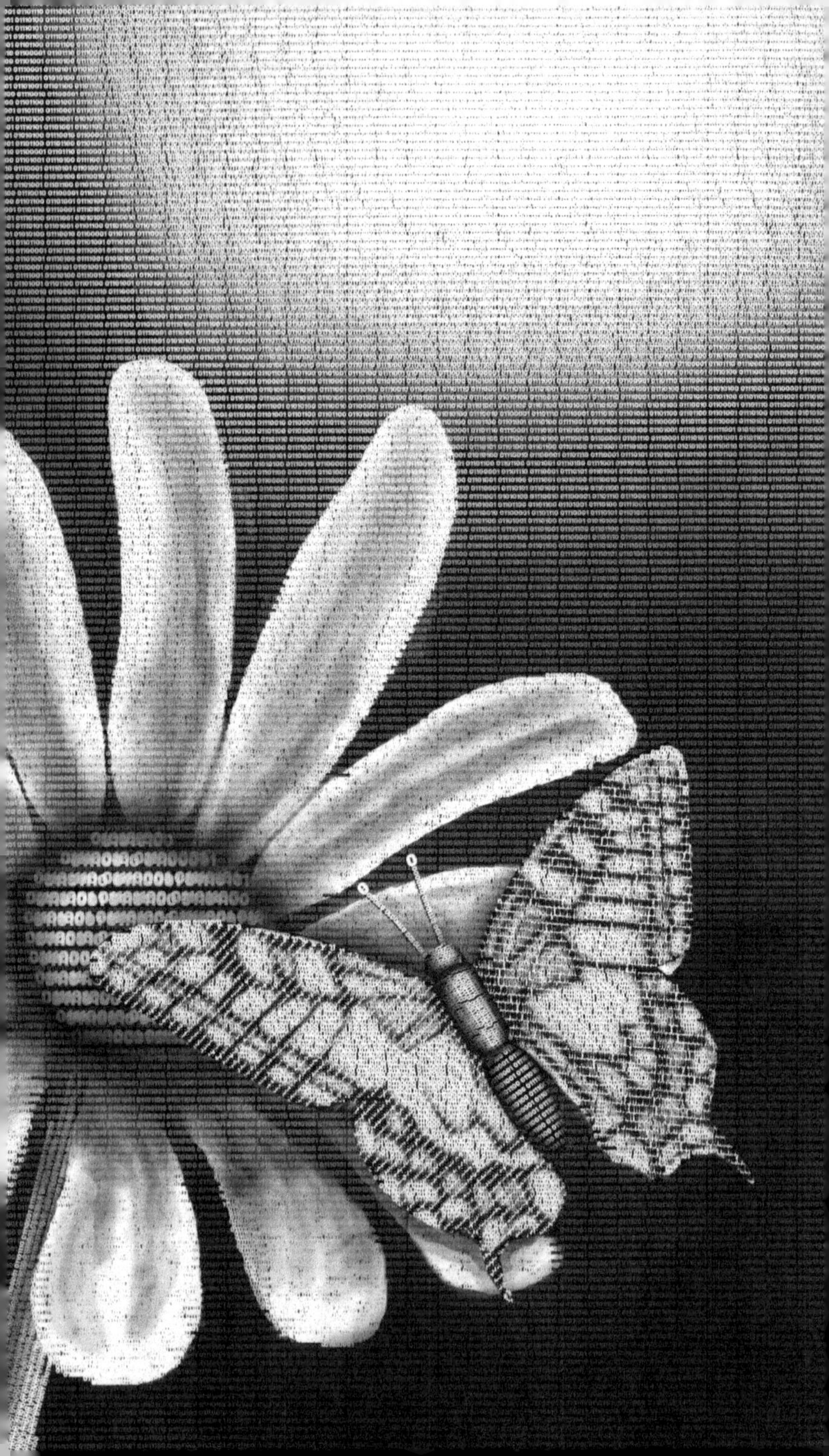

Chapter 11
Is this her world?

I stumbled and then tumbled to a cold, hard floor. When I dared to open my eyes and stand, I wasn't outside the dungeon, or even back in the sepia streets that had been my torment for so long. I was in a large bright, white train station, with people hustling past. In the sky there were small capsules with papers inside, flying, darting around the people this way and that. Sleek bubble-shaped trains softly glided to a stop. Their doors opened with a swish as they gently bobbed in thin air, like boats on an unseen water. People dashed out of the carriages, and others stepped inside, followed by the capsules of paper. The brightness and clinical finish of everything left me squinting a little. What's more, the people here seemed very different from the ones in the dungeon or even in the sepia streets. Their clothing all seemed unique, full of colour and flamboyance. Some strode in human-like forms, others had wings, wheels, or even multiple legs to get around. Some even seemed an odd mix of creatures. But they bustled about, intently immersed in their own thoughts, focused on going somewhere, or presumably doing something.

"Kentaro," a gentle voice whispered close by. "It is ok, you are safe now."

I turned to see Felicia standing right there next to me. Not separated by cruel glass, or helping me fleetingly, but there, standing leisurely, gently smiling. Right there, so close. My heart leapt in sheer delight. And suddenly a plethora of emotions seized my body. I tried to rationalise my mind, using only logic, but logic was long gone. The ogre and the guardians flashed before my mind, and I shuddered in fear, then the excitement of Felicia being by me made me feel elation. Then fear, joy, confusion, and so many more undefinable feelings all refused to wait their turn and demanded to be expressed. My hold on them gave way. I dropped to the floor and wept uncontrollably, my body convulsing. It was too much, I had held on, focused on escaping for so long.

"Felicia," I managed to mumble, between sobs.

"It is ok, Kentaro. You are free."

Her consoling words only brought more feeling. The word 'free' suddenly erupted in my heart and I wept harder.

"Hey, it's ok to cry," Felicia said. "You have been through so much, but you are safe now."

Her acceptance helped me and I let myself feel and process those things: a raging river of feeling like I had never known before. I sobbed and sobbed, moving through each emotion. And all the time she sat beside me, her warm, brown eyes filling with tears too, and gently nodding.

Eventually, after working through wave after wave, I began to settle down and was able to regain control over my body. Something seemed odd though, as I dried my eyes, I felt lighter, and more balanced.

"Hey, I think you needed that, dear Kentaro," she said, with that smile that never ceased to stir my heart.

"Felicia, I have missed you." I said, while standing. "I don't know how you reached into my dark world and rescued me, but you did." I looked into her eyes and smiled.

"I have missed you too," she said, her eyes meeting mine. "It wasn't easy getting you out, and for a moment, I thought

I had lost you forever. But what matters is that you are safe now," she explained.

"What is this place?" I asked, suddenly remembering we were standing in a busy station. "Is this your world? It is so colourful and wonderous."

"Let's grab this train. I will tell you all about this place later. But first, I have something to show you. Follow me, dear Kentaro," she said, holding out her hand.

I held out mine too, mimicking, not quite sure what to do. Suddenly I felt the warm touch of her hand on mine. The alien sensation sent my heart pounding, and I looked up at her. She smiled lovingly and we lost ourselves for a moment as our eyes met.

"Follow me," she said, gently tugging at my hand, a grin on her face.

And she led me across the platform, but it was all a blur, for all I could think of was the fact that we were holding hands, and actually together.

A train bobbed to a standstill, and when the doors whooshed open, we got on.

The train moved effortlessly. Gently swaying from side to side, we watched from the window together as a beautiful city flashed by. I could just make out its high, domed towers and the vibrant colourful streets. I turned to look at Felicia, her hair was just as stunning as ever, but had fallen into her eyes. I reached up to brush it away and we found ourselves lost in each other's gaze again. My heart was a flutter, and for the first time in my life I felt like I truly had no worries. I was free and with the only person I would want to share that freedom with. We stood, unaware of anything but each other, even time. Suddenly the train had stopped and the door slid open. We emerged from our dream-like state and she led me off onto a tiny village platform.

I looked around to see who else had gotten off, to find that we were standing alone, swirls of dust dancing as the train moved off, giving way to a soft silence. I felt a tug at my hand and followed Felicia as she led me down a few steps to a lush, green field. On the other side of the field we came to a gate, which she tapped a tune on with her fingers and it swung open. Beyond was the quaintest little park I have ever known. Surrounded by the seclusion of lines of trees, there were rows of flowers neatly set out, and right in the centre an ancient oak tree stood proud. Gently swaying in the breeze, a rope ladder led up the tree to a cozy-looking tree house. I felt the warm sun on my face, a feeling I had read about in books, but that felt far more wonderful in real life. I stood marvelling at it all, letting the sun's glow lighten my mood as I watched birds dart about the sky in frivolity. Squirrels bounded from branch to branch, and butterflies fluttered from petal to petal. I felt so very alive, in that wonderful park, it soothed the grey, ochre-toned memories of the world I had come from. And what is more, it filled me with hope knowing that not everywhere was like my world.

We gently pattered across the lush lawn together and sat on the grass. I lay back, letting the softness pillow my head and ran my fingers through grass and she did the same. We stayed there in silence listening to entrancing bird song. A few wispy clouds drifted in, and to my confusion, Felicia pointed at one and said, "Look, a dragon!"

"What," I cried in fear, sitting up. "Where?"

"No, not a real one, don't panic, Kentaro," she chuckled. "The cloud, it is shaped like a dragon".

I stared, trying to work out how a cloud could resemble a dragon.

"Look, there is the head, and those wispy bits either side are the wings," she explained.

I half closed my eyes and allowed my mind to draw lines around it; sure enough, it did. "Yes, I see it!" I exclaimed. Just then, I noticed another wispy cloud and to my utter surprise, my mind, without command, began to imagine that it looked like an old man bent over on a stick. And what was more, my mouth seemed to be defiant too, and I was shouting, "Look, an old man with a walking stick."

Felicia snickered. "And that one looks like a dolphin," she declared, pointing to another. I followed her finger to a delightfully shaped cloud that appeared to be just like a dolphin bounding through a vast ocean in the sky.

We sat there for what seemed like hours looking for shapes in the sky, lost, together, in a game that felt so new to me, yet so delightful. There were so many shapes that came and went as we giggled at them. When the warmth of the day began to fade, and the game had begun to tire, we simmered down. I turned to Felicia and smiled, she smiled back, and I felt her fingers entwine in mine.

"I could stay here forever with you," I uttered, awaiting her response expectantly.

"Me too," she said, a slight look of concern. "You are safe here, dear Kentaro," she said, softly. "This will be our park."

"Is this your home?" I asked. "Where you live."

"No, Kentaro it isn't. But it is our special place now," she said.

"Won't other people come here?" I asked, confused.

"No, only we can use this place. I designed ..." she started, but was interrupted by a buzzing on her wrist. I felt the vibrations tingle through my fingers too.

She looked gently into my eyes and smiled. "I would love to stay here with you forever, but I have to go. I will be back later and we can be together again."

I felt sad at the thought of her leaving after we had only

just been united, having been through so much pain and darkness, just to find that she wasn't staying.

"Hey," she said, noticing my sadness. "I am coming back later, I promise."

"Ok," I said, trying to regulate my emotions. "Where are you going?" I asked.

"I have things to do. But you have everything you need here. If you want to sleep or rest, you can stay in the tree house," she said, touching my shoulder.

"When will you be back?"

"Late tonight, or very early tomorrow," she replied, a slight sadness in her eyes.

Another buzz erupted from her wrist and as she stood to walk away, our fingers pulled apart. At the gate, she turned to look back at me and smiled, our eyes met for a brief moment, before she turned away. Wiping a few tears, I watched as she disappeared towards the bright lights of the station, then she was gone.

And then I was alone. Something that had once seemed like an old, familiar friend somehow now seemed less welcome. I had found out what it was to spend time with someone, I had tasted the sweetness of company. I lay back replaying our afternoon together, reliving each moment, cherishing it. I felt warm and at ease as I relived the moments, while listening to the birdsong. Just then though, rudely, images of the guardians, and the prisoners, and that terrifying ogre flashed before me, followed by the ochre streets of that world from which I had escaped. I tried to calm myself and opened my eyes. To my relief, I was still lying in the safety of the beautiful park. I closed my eyes again and tried to process the events of the day. So much had changed. I had begun my day as a prisoner but was now free. Free from the terror of my world, from the reaches of IO, from the touch of the whip, and most of all, from the grey monotony of the workhouse. But, there was more to freedom than just place. I was now free to be me, the man, the person, I wanted to be. Excited about the possibilities, I opened my eyes and sat up, only to see something strange. Something I had only read about in books: a sunset. The sky was ablaze with its fire, and the birds erupted into a crescendo of chorus. It was truly magnificent, beyond the description of the words in the books. But just as quickly as it had started it was over, and soon, it was dark. So I lay back wondering where my freedom would take me next…

CLOTHING
VERSE

Chapter 12
Clothingverse

I awoke with sunlight pouring into my eyes. A warm smile further lit my world as I gazed into Felicia's eyes.

"You are back," I declared. "Where did you go?"

"I had things to do," she said, looking away. When she looked back she smiled. "But I missed you, Kentaro."

"I missed you too," I found myself saying. "Did you have a nice night?" I enquired.

"It was busy, but ok. I had to finish a few assignments and do one or two architectural jobs. Glad to be back though." She stood up and glanced at the tree house. "Why didn't you sleep up there?" she asked.

"I don't really know, I was just enjoying the park and then I watched the sunset… Felicia, it was so beautiful. I have never seen anything quite like it before."

She grinned. "There is a perfect view of it from here isn't there, that is why there is a gap in the treeline there," she said, pointing it out. "I knew you would like it."

I stood, my body ached a little after the arduous escape the day before. Felicia stood too, looking me up and down strangely. "Your grey clothes are so dull," she declared.

"Really?" I asked, peering down at them.

"Yes, come and look for yourself in the mirror," she said, her hand grabbing mine and pulling me in the direction of the tree house. We climbed the rope ladder, far, far up the old oak. To my surprise, and Felicia's, I was fast and nimble on the ladder dashing up it. We emerged at the top, in front of the door, on a small, fenced balcony. I reached out for the brass handle and opened the door. It swung neatly inwards to reveal a massive room. I tentatively stepped inside to find myself bemused by just how big it was.

"Why is it so much bigger than it looks outside?" I asked.

"Ah, it is all down to efficient design," she explained. "It has everything. Including a mirror," she said, tugging my hand towards the far side, where a mirror hung on the wall.

I looked at my reflection, and became more aware of my sense of self. I smiled, shifted and moved, playfully enjoying the novelty of my own reflection. Felicia chortled watching me.

"I guess you didn't have mirrors in ..." She let the question trail off, a worried look in her eyes. "Sorry, didn't mean to remind you of that place," she said, softly.

"It's ok," I said. "It *was* a horrible place, but it was also where I first met you," I added, smiling. "I used to try to see my reflection in the windows between your visits."

"And what do you see now?" she asked.

I stepped back a little to see my whole self. "Well, I see a someone!" I said, with a grin!

"What, in those grey rags?" she asked.

"Hey, it isn't the clothing that makes me – me!" I declared.

"No, very true, but we can express ourselves through our clothing," she said.

"I have read about such things, but I am not sure how that works."

She stepped a little closer and ran her hand through my green hair.

"Your hair is so expressive. But what about these grey rags, are they an expression of yourself?"

"No" I gasped, understanding suddenly. "No, they express the world I used to be in, the life I was forced to live. I actually hate them!"

"Well Kentaro, let's do something about that!" And at that, she turned and walked towards the front door.

"Where are you going?" I asked.

"You will see!" she said, with a grin. "Come on."

I followed her back down the ladder and across the park to the station.

Not long after arriving at the station a train stopped and we got on. It was quite empty so we sat down together, gently rocking to the sway of the train. Suddenly, our peaceful moment was interrupted by a rude woman.

"Hey, you need to update your personal details," she said, holding out a clipboard and a pen.

Felicia looked sternly at the woman and shook her head.

"Don't tell her anything," she whispered. We both ignored her and eventually the woman gave up and moved onto some other people.

We watched as people walked past, getting on and off the train at various places. Everyone was *so* vibrant, their clothing so expressive, their features and bodies diverse. Even Felicia seemed entranced by watching the characters coming and going. Eventually, the train stopped at a gigantic, bright station. There were rows and rows of tracks all below a curved glass roof. As I stepped off the train, I felt the energy of the station wash over me. It was the busiest place I had ever been to.

I felt Felicia pull at my hand. "This way," she said. "Don't lose me here. It is a big place. So stay close." We scurried through the crowds of people and other beings, dashing around, between, and sometimes even under, them. Coming to a set of barriers, she tapped her fingers on them and they slid open to let us both pass. On the other side, a truly massive station was revealed, complete with a classic clock - way above. There were creatures, beings, and peoploids everywhere. Some in groups chatting and laughing. Others were waiting on benches. And there were a few that stood alone, strangely speaking to themselves. But it soon became a blur as Felicia and I traversed the scene swiftly. We slowed and then stepped onto an escalator, which took us high above the station to another floor. When we stepped off, we were in a mall. Bright shopfronts lined each side, advertising every conceivable thing. Some of which I recognised, and others I didn't. Eventually, after lots more meandering we came to a brightly coloured glass door.

"What is this this place?" I asked.

"Welcome to Clothingverse! Kentaro," she said dramatically, as we stepped through the slick doors.

I looked around, but I couldn't see any clothing, just a brightly lit space. Suddenly, when we got halfway in, the walls flashed into life, with a grand display of people walking and moving in a variety of costumes. The costumes flickered and merged from colour to colour, and from style to style. I stopped, overwhelmed by the bright commercials I was surrounded by. I found myself flitting from wall to wall, unable to truly settle and engage with one advert, but completely consumed.

"Don't stop, you will be here for hours watching those adverts," Felicia said. But I was already too engrossed to reply. All I could manage was a mumbled "Yeeeah" as I stared.

Just then, Felicia abruptly stood in front of me, her face pulling me out of the lush advert display.

"Hey," she said, looking directly into my eyes. "Remember me?" She smiled.

"Ah," I said, suddenly feeling very ashamed. "You weren't kidding when you said not to stop. It is so addictive watching those adverts."

"This way," she said, her head nodding to the side.

I followed her over to a door, making an effort to not get pulled back into the lush, vivid wall-show around me. On the other side of the door, we arrived at a series of massive rooms. Each room had seating along one side pointing towards a large, curved wall. The rest of the room was empty flooring, covered in a soft carpet.

The lights dimmed to a soft yellow and for a moment I imagined I was back in the darkness of the workhouse, or worse. I shuddered, looking around in fear of IO arriving, or that terrifying ogre from the dungeon. It suddenly felt hard to breathe too and I found myself gasping for breath.

"Hey!" Felicia said, in a soft voice, putting her hand on my shoulder. "You are safe. Look at *me* Kentaro, try to take slow breaths."

Her words helped to bring me back a little, her soft gentle eyes cut through the panic and slowly I managed to calm myself, focusing on the fact that that world was behind me now.

Just then, the lights brightened and a rather cheerful looking old man arrived in the doorway. "Welcome to Clothingverse," he announced. "Where your expression is our passion." He smiled at Felicia and then looked at me. His eyes widened and he raised an eyebrow. "Grey?" he declared. "How very unusual. I like the distressing on it too, it looks very realistic."

I didn't know what to say to this, and was just contemplating the truth, when Felicia saved me from embarrassment.

"Yes, they are good at the destressed look nowadays,

aren't they? But we are here for a change!" she briskly said, looking me in the eye.

"Very good," the old man said, while straightening a measuring tape that hung around his neck. "Feel free to peruse our range. You won't find a better one … anywhere!" he announced, proudly. "How would you like to browse the aisles?"

"Give me voice command please," Felicia asked.

"No problem. And would you like assistance or to browse alone?"

"Browsing alone would be good," Felicia declared.

"Very good. Just call if you need anything," he said, bowing slightly to us both, and then he left, shutting the door behind himself.

Felicia grinned at me. "So, Kentaro, what do you fancy?" she asked.

I had no idea what to say. I just stood there staring at her, trying to make sense of clothing being a choice. "I … I just don't know. I have never been given a choice about clothing before. What have they got?" I enquired.

"Kentaro dear, they have EVERYTHING."

"Everything, surely not?"

"No, really they do. If you can think of it, they have it!" she said firmly.

"I don't believe that. I bet they haven't got pirate clothing," I challenged.

"Oh, come on, Kentaro. Of course they have. Historical, or fantasy?"

I refused to believe Felicia, so thought I would put it to the test. "Historical. Have they got Golden Age clothing from the 1600s?"

"Oh please!" she said, rolling her eyes. "Clothingverse give me the 1600s pirate section."

There was a whooshing sound and instantly rows and rows of clothing appeared in the room and the walls became reflective like mirrors. We wandered down several aisles; I was amazed by all the rich velvet garments, tricorn hats, racks of cutlasses, and regalia. I reached out for a particularly beautiful red velvet coat, but my fingers passed through it.

"It isn't real," I declared. "And there is only one size for everything."

"Ask for one while trying to touch it, and as for sizes, it is adaptive sizing," she said, a mischievous grin erupting on her face.

"Ok," I said tentatively. I reached out to touch the red one and said in a clear voice, "Can I have this?" Suddenly, I was adorned in the coat. I looked up to see the rich fabric flowing around me perfectly and the golden edging sparkling. "Wow," I shouted in surprise. Confused, I wondered if I was still sleeping in the park and perhaps this was all a fantastical dream.

"Oh I say, you do look dashing in that," Felicia said, suddenly arriving in front of me dressed in equally impressive pirate gear, complete with cutlass. I stumbled back in surprise, tripping over, knocking my elbow on the way down. It hurt, or at least the pain certainly felt real, so I ruled out dreaming. I scrambled to stand and we both chuckled.

"Is that real?" I asked, noticing how sharp the cutlass looked.

"Let's find out," she replied, gesturing to a rack full of weapons.

I selected a rather heavily jewel-encrusted sword and said, "This, please." The sword rather abruptly appeared attached to my right side by a belt.

"Well, Kentaro, let's see what you have got?" Felicia said, drawing her sword.

I drew mine too and held it out in front of me, unsure how to really use it.

"Take a swing at me," she said.

"Nope!" I refused. "I might hurt you."

"So you agree it is real then."

"I am not so sure … but I don't want to chance it."

"Weapon test please," Felicia announced, and there was a whoosh as the clothing aisles slid away and the room was filled with targets, and training dummies.

"Thought this was just a clothing store?" I asked.

"It is, but they also have a large stock of accessories and facilities to test them. Now, swing your sword at that straw dummy over there," she said, raising her eyebrows. "Go on, you won't hurt it."

I dashed over with the excitement of being able to try the sword. Stopping in front of it, my large frame the same height, I narrowed my eyes and swung the sword with everything I had. There was a cloud of dust and straw as the blade cut through it, and then it slipped out of my sweaty hands. I rushed over to pick it up, eyeing the pristine edge in excitement.

"It is so sharp," I declared, excitedly bringing my finger to touch the blade. Barely touching it, to my horror, I felt it slice through the skin on my finger. "Ah," I muttered, as blood ran down my finger and the wound started to sting.

"Kentaro," Felicia said. "What are you doing? Never touch the blade." She dashed over, producing a small tube of liquid and managed to close the wound by sticking it. "You are lucky it's a clean cut. But we might need to keep you away from weapons, from now on."

"Weapon test finished," she announced, and then the room became empty again. I looked down at the red coat and over to her pirate clothing.

"Not sure these clothes are exactly us," I said.

She touched the sword and said, "I don't need this." It disappeared. Then we both did the same with our other clothing and I found myself back in my grey rags.

"Ok, so what kind of clothing should we try next?" Felicia asked.

"I don't know," I said.

"Please show us some recommendations," she commanded.

There was another whoosh, followed by a massive selection of all sorts of things. We began walking down the aisles, stopping to laugh at many of the odd costumes. There was clothing from every period of history, in every colour imaginable. Halfway down an aisle I stopped, spotting a particularly over the top item. "This please," I announced, turning to see it in the mirror. The garment had swirls of yellow fabric that started on my shoulders and flowed down, upon hitting the floor, they curled around into giant features. I could suddenly barely move in its ridiculous flamboyance.

"What do you think of this?" I asked Felicia.

She burst out into uncontrollable laughter, followed by me. I doubled over, heaving as I laughed so much, the dress catching beneath my feet and causing me to flop on the floor in a big ball of yellow fabric. She rushed over, still wheezing in frivolity, reaching out her hand to try to get me up. But she also got caught up in the dress and fell, and we ended up tangled in each other's arms and in the dress, mere inches from one another. I found myself caught in her gaze, enchanted in a moment that I never wanted to end. The room slipped away, everything becoming hazy around me, all except her. She lent in and for a tiny moment, her lips touched my cheek in a kiss. Then she rolled off and stood up. But there I remained, lost in what had just happened.

That tiny moment, that tiny gesture, left me changed. I could still feel her lips on my cheek, my heart racing, ablaze in elation, and my mind a whirlwind of thoughts I was trying to understand. I brought my hand to my cheek to touch the place where she had kissed it. Looking up, I saw her gentle smile and clambered to my feet.

We laughed our way through the day, as we tried on so many clothes, from the absurd to the stiflingly boring. As we explored how they made us feel and look we imagined the type of person that might wear them, putting on voices to imitate them, which just made us laugh all the more. I felt strangely contented and the horrors of my old life finally seemed further away than they had ever been. I was totally at ease, drifting through the endless blissful day, cherishing every moment with Felicia. It had been the longest I had ever spent with her yet, though she was someone I would never tire of being with. We brought out the best in each other and time passed so quickly when we were together. But then I found myself wondering if it would last.

We left the Clothingverse late afternoon with so many bags of clothes that we had to use 6 seats on the train home. I sat admiring my rich orange shirt and baggy trousers in the window reflection. Strangely, I *did* feel more *me* now – on the outside that was. It felt good to not be wearing the grey reminders of the workhouse anymore. When I had gone to leave, they had put them in a bag, but I asked for them to be discarded. When I saw them drop into that bin, I felt like the last piece of my old life had been let go of, I felt like I was finally ready to accept my new life. I realised that Felicia had been right, the clothing we wear can be an extension of ourselves. I glanced at the plump bags filled with an eclectic mix of clothes, mostly for me, but some for her too, and I grinned.

Dashing up to the tree house we put the clothing down and decided to catch the sunset together. We sat holding hands, the perfect end to a perfect day. I never thought it was possible to feel so happy, to *be* so very happy. But having my own freedom and spending time with Felicia had proved me wrong. I wished that day and that moment would never end, but sadly the bitter fact of life is that nothing lasts forever, no matter how dearly beautiful or truly pure it is. All moments must fade. And, as the first stars came out in the inky sky, I heard the cruel buzz from her wrist. She stood to leave. But just before she turned, she kissed me on the cheek.

"I will be back soon, my dear Kentaro," she said, and then she was gone.

SNAIL LAND
DRAGON
SNAIL
LAND
DRAGON

Chapter 13
Where do you go to?

It took me a while to fall asleep that night. I could still feel her lips on my cheek, I could hardly wait till she came back the next day. I must have slept eventually though, because I awoke to find here sitting beside me on the tree house bed.

"Good morning, Kentaro," she softly whispered. "Did you sleep okay?"

"Yes, but I don't remember when, or even getting into bed," I said. "How was your evening?"

"It was busy," she replied. "I had lots to do."

"Where do you go in the evenings?" I asked. "I mean, where *is* your house? Can I see where you live?" She looked away. And when she looked back she tried to smile, but I could see she was fighting something.

"Let's have a lovely day together first," she said. "I promise I will tell you more later, and if you really want to see where I live, I will show you." Her eyes glazed over slightly at the last few words. I wanted to ask more, and find out what was bothering her. It saddened me to think that something was on her mind. I tried to formulate a sentence that would be loving and supportive, but that would allow her to feel safe to share her troubles. But my emotions kept getting in the way.

"Hey," she said, looking deep into my eyes. "I promise, we'll talk about it later. But please let's just have a nice day first. I want it to be perfect!"

I gently nodded, submitting. How could I ever disagree with dear Felicia, she was my everything. I would go to the ends of the world and back for her if she asked. I would slay a monster or even wait a lifetime if she would but give me a smile.

She stood up and took my hand and together we climbed down from the tree house. The early morning sun had painted the park in golden hues, and the first of the butterflies were flitting from flower to flower.

"It is a beautiful morning," she said, holding my hand. And we stood for a moment hand in hand, close to one another, wrapped in silence, just listening to the trees and park around us.

"So, Kentaro," Felicia finally said, breaking the silence. "Are you in the mood for an adventure and some action?"

"Always," I said. "So what is on the menu?"

"Well, in this amazing world we can do literally anything! How about kicking off with some games?"

"What kind of games?" I asked, but she was already pulling me towards the park exit.

"You will see," she chanted, and we were off.

We caught a train, which gently pulled up to a platform next to a gigantic dome. The dome was covered in bright lights and images. We dashed down towards the entrance and through some double doors.

Inside, it was a lot darker, with neon acrid lights glowing along the floor and thousands of rows of machines flashing. She dashed down an aisle to a rather retro-looking one with two round joy pads and a flickering screen.

"Oh yeah," Felicia announced. "This is one of my favourites."

I looked at the grainy, flickering screen and could make

out dune buggies darting over sand. I grabbed the joy pad, and wiggled it. But nothing happened.

"Got to push 'Start', Kentaro," she said, with a wink.

I hit 'Start'. The room went black, and for a moment, I felt a little nausea. Moments later, I was standing in the roasting sun next to a dune buggy.

"What are you waiting for?" Felicia called from inside another buggy, while she aggressively revved the engine and edged it forward.

I jumped into the buggy and soon familiarised myself with the controls. The accelerator was lively though, and it flung me backwards in my seat.

"See ya," Felicia chided, leaving me in a cloud of dust. But I wasn't going to let her get away. So I kicked the accelerator down hard and tried to keep the machine in a straight line. I got the hang of it quickly, and seemed to be catching her up. Just as she slid around a corner, I took the inside line, almost rolling it, but managed to slip past her on 2 wheels.

"See ya," I shouted, quite pleased with myself. But it seemed I had underestimated her, because moments later she had sped past me giggling to herself. I drove hard, but she was not going to let me overtake again. Every time I got close, she blocked my way, and then hit the boost, leaving me in the dust. When we finished several laps, I came to a stop at the finish line to find her already out of her buggy.

"Did you stop for a picnic?" she asked.

"No! … I, I." But I gave up. She had me and she knew it. "All right, you beat me. But I will win the next game."

"Oh, really?" she questioned. "Well, as the loser, you can name the game."

Suddenly, we were back in the games room, in front of the console.

I strode down the banks of consoles till a cool street racer caught my eye. "This one," I said, and not even waiting for her to arrive, I hit the start. I found myself standing next to a large selection of cars in a garage. There were classic muscle cars, Japanese drifters, and even supercars.

"Nice collection," Felicia said, from behind me. "You choose first, dear Kentaro," she said softly.

"I will take the metallic green Japanese drifter. How about you?"

I will take the same, but in black!" she said. "Matte black."

We got in the cars, and sped out of the garage leaving skid marks and a thick cloud of smoke hanging in the air.

At the lights, we revved our engines playfully at each other. The lights flashed green, and Felicia blew me a kiss.

"See you at the finish line… in second place," she teased, and then she roared up the track.

"Not if I can help it," I muttered. I dropped the hammer and sped down the track after her. As the scenery whizzed by, I realised that the track was actually set out on streets running around a town. I hustled hard to try to catch her up - she was really good. But I felt determined to not lose *this* time. She might be my dear Felicia, the one person in the whole world that I loved, but this was a serious game and I was going to win. I pushed harder and harder taking chances, finding the very edge of the car's limits, and soon I was on her back bumper constantly fighting to get past. Then, just as we were approaching the sharpest corner, I decided to not brake early and tried to slip by her. She slowed down, sliding into a drift, but I held the speed just that bit longer. I had to get past her, at any cost. Suddenly, the corner was upon me, though, and I couldn't get round it. A massive concrete side block was approaching me. I was going to hit it and hit it hard. "I love you Felicia," I uttered, knowing I was probably not going to walk away from an impact that bad. I closed my eyes, tensed, the concrete image refusing to leave my mind. I screwed up my face, my body taught. But nothing came. When I opened my eyes, I was on another part of the track, regaining control. I yanked the wheel to get back in a straight line, and continued driving. I saw no sign of Felicia, though, not until I looked in my rear view mirror; she was a tiny dot.

I hit the finish line, a little confused, but feeling rather smug to be first. I got out of my car and sat on the bonnet for her to catch up and finish the race.

"What took you so long? Did you stop for a four-course meal?" I said, giggling from my comfy position on the car. She gave me a playful scowl and we dropped out of the game.

Back in the games arena, Felicia put her arm around me and we walked silently for a moment looking for the next game.

"Nice driving, Kentaro!" Felicia agreed. "Though I can't work out how you managed to get past me."

I pondered what to say and decided to simply go for "skills, my love, skills," in jest.

"OH, wow they have this game now," Felicia declared, pointing to a flame-red console. "Oh, Kentaro, you are going to LOVE this game."

I should have looked at the console, but I just hit 'Start', getting swept up in Felicia's excitement.

I was suddenly standing on the top of a mountain, but something was wrong, the floor looked a long way away. I moved my arm, but instead of my arm a clumsily large red wing came into view. Inspecting my body, I realised I was no longer Kentaro, but a scaly dragon. "What's happened?" I shouted.

"It is okay, my dear. I am a dragon too. And remember it is just a game," Felicia growled from an equally fierce-looking dragon standing in front of me.

"Oh, right. Of course," I said, feeling a little silly.

"Follow me!" she said, and she dove off the mountainside, her wings majestically allowing her to sail on the wind. I did the same, which was a massive adrenaline rush because I failed to open my wings, so I found myself twisting and plummeting towards the valley below. Fearful of the ground getting rapidly closer, I opened my wings and with a sudden jolt I jerked back and was left gliding on the wind. A rush of excitement and elation filled my body, as I soared gracefully above towns, forests, and rivers. Felicia had circled around and was now flying with me. Together we sped through the air, our hearts pumping. We dropped down just above the treetops of a verdant forest. I could feel the soft new leaves brushing against me. I could smell the pine scent from below, mixed with a moist mulch. We pulled up and then instantly were meandering between the clouds. Pulling up again, we found ourselves in a wonderous landscape, with the clouds below now a fluffy carpet and the vivid blue sky arcing on either side.

"Bet you can't catch me!" I suddenly declared, getting carried away by the playful nature of being a dragon. I dropped out of the clouds, flapping my wings hard, followed by Felicia. She heaved to try to keep up, but I was so full of adrenalin I was flying to the full, darting around trees, and then up to the rocky cliffs. Spotting a gap between two massive boulders, I decided to dare fly between them. I knew it would impress Felicia, so I took aim and brought my wings in like an arrow. I flew straight and true but my pride had gotten the better of me, and I had misjudged the gap. It was too narrow. I pulled up trying to evade it. Narrowly missing the rocks, I caught a tree branch which put me into a spin, crashing down in a woodland. I managed to scramble to my feet, the tall trees looming above me. My wings and body stung a bit, but I was ok.

Just then, behind me I heard a branch snap, spinning around I saw several large wolves. Turning back, to my dismay, I realised more wolves had now cornered me. Scanning around for a way out, I saw they had me hemmed in. Their snarling got louder and they readied to pounce. Fear racked my body as I imagined them ripping me to pieces. I closed my eyes, but they were still there in my mind, but they looked different somehow. I heard their snarling get louder and Felicia cry as they pounced. I tensed, awaiting their sharp teeth piercing my body all over. Then, the snarling turned to a strange, soft whimpering. I opened my eyes, and before me were baby wolf pups, rolling around in the undergrowth playfully. Felicia was standing a little way off with a look of confusion on her face. She gestured for us to leave, and we exited the game.

Back in the games arena Felicia gasped in shock. Looking at me with a strange and suspicious look.

"Hey, what did you do in that game, you changed the game?" she uttered.

I had no idea what she was talking about. I just felt a little sick with all the jumping from game to game. That, and the whole wolves encounter.

"Do it again, Kentaro. Change me into a wolf cub," Felicia said, her face not betraying her surprise.

"That is impossible. I don't know what I did, and besides, it was only a game."

"But you changed those wolves," she said. "I saw you do it. Change me, go on."

"Don't be silly, Felicia; it was just a game. This is the real world; I can't change you into a wolf, any more than I can turn into a dragon and fly off into the sunset."

"I suppose you are right, Kentaro. It must have been a

glitch," she said. "What's next?"

We whiled away many more hours that day playing so many different games, including battle games, sim games and even a great first-person fantasy, where she played an elf and I played a wizard. We got completely lost in that land, it was so vast that we eventually gave up and said we would come back another day, just to play it. Next, we had a coffee in a quaint little café in the back streets of an idyllic town. We wandered around the cobbled streets window shopping, completely lost in our own world, giggling at everything like children.

It was mid-afternoon by the time we left the town and I thought we might be heading home, back to the tree house. But then we took another train in a different direction.

"Where are we going?" I asked.

"There is one more place I would like to show you today," Felicia declared.

"Wow, there is so much to do here. Where are we headed?"

"You will have to wait and … see," she said, playfully. So I just went with it.

I felt her hand slip into mine as the train pulled up and we picked our way through crowds of others. We dashed off the platform and towards a modern-looking glass building. It was clean-lined and fairly bland, other than a larger than life sign that read 'Travelverse an Infocorp company'. The word 'Infocorp' seemed to feel familiar to me, but no matter how hard I tried to rack my brain, I could not work out why. I paused, looking at the words, caught in a flurry of thought.

"Hey, the fun is inside, my love. Not here, come on," Felicia said, eagerly pulling at my hand.

"Yes … of course," I muttered. "Sorry," I said, pulling myself away from the annoying mystery.

As we walked through the sliding doors we were greeted by a smartly dressed lady.

"Welcome to Travelverse," she said, with just a little too much excitement. "Is it your first time travelling with us?"

"No, I have been lots of times before," Felicia said. "Though it is his first time."

"Welcome back miss," she said, bowing, then looked at me. "Enjoy your first time," she said, cheerfully, holding my gaze for just a little too long for it to be comfortable. I nodded politely and walked away arm in arm with Felicia.

"Wait here, I will be back in a moment," she said, and dashed off towards a service counter, where she became quickly engrossed in an animated conversation with a staff member.

"Excuse me sir," a soft voice said from behind me. I spun round to see the lady from the front door smiling at me.

"Hi again," I said.

"As it is your first time here, I wondered if you would accept these cookies?" she said, handing me a small pack of a few very nicely decorated cookies. Each one had the name 'Travelverse' printed on it.

"Oh, thank you. That is really kind of you," I said, returning the smile. I slipped the small packet into my pocket.

"Enjoy your travels with us," the lady said, and moved off to tend to some other people who were arriving.

Several moments later Felicia was back with a very large grin. "Kentaro dear, you are going to love this," she said. "Follow me". She led me to a wall completely lined with doors. The wall stretched on as far as the eye could see in both directions. Every door was identical - simple, white and sturdy, but bland. The only discerning characteristic was the number above each one. Felicia looked at a strip of paper in her hand, comparing it to the numbers, and after wandering up and down the wall several times, we found the corresponding door.

"Go ahead, Kentaro," she said. "You go first."

I opened the door and was instantly hit by a strange, salty smell. I peered inside, but it was dark, so I tentatively stepped through the doorway. Suddenly, I found myself on a golden, sandy beach. It was beautiful, but taking another step, the sand felt a little frightening. I could feel it dragging me down, pulling at my feet. Darkness and screams started flashing in my mind.

"Hey," Felicia said, catching my worried gaze. Her gentle smile and loving eyes calmed me. The sunshine returned and I saw the turquoise sea lapping gently at the shore.

"Isn't it wonderful, Kentaro," Felicia said. She was wearing shorts, sandals, and a t-shirt. I checked in with my own clothing, sure that we had not left the tree house with extra clothes, and was amazed to see I too was wearing matching attire.

Felicia kicked off her sandals and dashed to the shoreline. I followed her, abruptly stopping short of the waves. I felt a little apprehensive. I had read about the sea, but it seemed … well … wetter that it had done in books. But Felicia didn't have the same reticence, she dashed straight in, the waves splashing on her legs. She let out a contented sigh and stood there with the water around her knees. I kicked off my shoes too, and stepped forward. I stepped right up to the wet line on the sand, then I put a foot ever so slightly into the water. It felt cool and calming, soothing even, the sand swirling around my toes. I took another step and the other foot felt the same all over again. I ventured further, to my ankles, then to my knees, the soft water swirling around my legs, the sand shifting below my feet. I looked out at the sunlight bouncing off the jewel-like ocean. A few fluffy clouds drifted in the sky, and then my gaze fell on Felicia, who was watching me contentedly. A few tears fell from my eyes, at the awe and perfection of the moment. I gazed at her, and she smiled. That gentle smile - that gentle smile that pulled me from my horrid, dull life in the workhouse - that smile that never ceased to lighten my heart. I waded closer and took her hands.

"Felicia," I said. "I love you so much."

"I love you too, so very much, Kentaro," she replied, her eyes filling with tears.

"This is truly the perfect end to the most perfect day spent together," I said, my eyes also filling with tears. "I wish this moment would never end."

"Me too, Kentaro," she said, stepping a little closer. Then she did something I wasn't expecting, she leaned in and kissed me on the lips. It was like the first time she had kissed me on the cheek all over again. A wave of emotion rushed through me. When she withdrew I could still feel her soft lips on mine. She giggled and turned away.

"Come on," she said, splashing through the water in a wade towards the wet sand. We ran down the beach, the soft sand crunching beneath our toes, and the sea washing over the tops of our feet. She slowed down and then stopped at part of the beach that had lots of stones. I reached down and picked one up, inspecting it. I noticed how smooth it was, how round, but slightly elongated. I picked another one up and it was identical. Felicia picked one up too, and then she did something that caught me off guard, she squatted down and then threw it towards the sea. Upon hitting the calm water, it bounced, skipping over the surface far, far out almost to the horizon.

"WOW!" I exclaimed in excitement. "How did you do that?"

"Skills, my dear love, skills!"

"Let me have a go," I declared, trying to mimic the action but just sending it plopping into the water.

"Look, hold it like this," she said, placing the stone in my hand and moving my arm to gesture the technique. I threw it, and it bounced once before splashing down. I practiced and practiced, and with her advice, eventually I managed to get the stone to spin and skip across the sea. But not quite so far and elegantly as Felicia could. When we had run out of enthusiasm for it, we wandered back arm in arm, the low sunset's glow dancing across the water. When we got back to the door, Felicia turned to me and brushed her hand against my cheek.

"Thank you for trusting me, Kentaro. Thank you for being in my life. Today *was* truly perfect," she said, and then she turned towards the door and stepped through.

On the other side of the door, I found myself dressed in my own clothing, dry and clean.

As we were leaving the Travelverse, heading towards the train station hand in hand, I felt that cruel buzz from her wrist cut through our moment. I looked down momentarily in sadness and annoyance. Why did she have to go? Our time together made me feel so very alive, and invigorated, yet every day she left me. Every time it felt like a bitter finish to an otherwise wonderful day. Maybe we could stay together. I could help her do her jobs, or she could maybe work from the park surely.

"Kentaro, I have to go," she said, forlornly.

"But, where? Where do you go every day? Why don't you stay? Or why don't I come with you?"

"You can't," she said, slightly raising her voice. "I am sorry. I mean, it is difficult."

"You said you would tell me where you go, or even show me where you live," I said, remembering her promise that morning. "Are you ashamed of me? A man that came from a workhouse, a drab world. Is that it?"

"NO!" she shouted. "How dare you even think that I would be ashamed of you?" She looked away in pain.

"I am sorry," I said, putting my hand tenderly on her shoulder. "I just don't understand why you leave every day. And when I ask about where you go, you avoid the subject."

She turned back, her eyes streaming with tears.

"It isn't your fault, dear, gentle Kentaro. It is my fault, I knew this day would come. But I hoped that it wouldn't."

"What do you mean? Are you breaking up with me?"

"No, not at all, never. But there are things about where I go. My world that is, that would tear us apart."

Shock and horror befell me. "Your world? What do you mean?" I asked, aghast. "I … I … thought this *was* your world," I said, now racked with confusion, my mind a flurry of thoughts.

Her head dropped in shame, and then she looked back at me. "Kentaro, this isn't my world, it's …" She let the sentence trail off and looked away, unable to finish.

"I don't care how different your world is, I don't care how difficult it will be. Nothing, nothing at all would, or could stop me from loving you, dear Felicia. Show me, trust me, and trust *us*."

"It isn't that simple, my love. You say you would not stop loving me now, but when you get there, it would tear us apart," she sighed.

"Look at what we have been through together, our love began in the darkness of looking through a dusty workhouse window. I trudged through pain and despair to be with you and you held on, guiding me, fighting for me to escape. We are strong, and our love is real. Show me, show me your world, and we will stand side by side together to overcome the differences."

"Kentaro, you just don't understand the differences of my world. But at the same time, you are right, I cannot keep avoiding this truth. It breaks my heart to leave you every day, to lie to you and to avoid the truth. I knew this day would come. I had hoped that we might get lost and distracted by being here, but alas if you must see my world, then so be it," she said.

I took her hand and pulled it close to my heart. "My dear Felicia. Our love is strong enough to endure. We will stand together and face this. No matter how different your world is, I will never ... never stop loving you. Show me, show me *your* world!"

She looked distraught, but nodded and mustered a smile. She took my hand and we walked silently the rest of the way to the station.

Chapter 14
Her world

We zapped through tunnels and across voids, watching all sorts of strange places unfold below us through the windows. Eventually, we got off the train at a boring-looking station that was deserted. She led me to a dusty window and suddenly disappeared.

I peered through the window and sitting in a swivel chair, staring at me, was Felicia. She was wearing shabby clothes, her hair was untidy and she looked tired, but it *was* her. As I peered in, she removed a pair of wraparound glasses with leads attached to them, to reveal those soft brown eyes I would know anywhere. She smiled at me, and I felt warm inside. She removed the black gloves with dim flashing lights she wore and lifted a hand to the window. I did the same.

"Is it really you?" I asked – She nodded, a stream of tears trickling down her face.

"How can I get through to join you, my dear?" I asked further, which caused her to only cry even more.

"I never wanted to hurt you, my dear Kentaro," she sobbed. "I just wanted to free you, but then the more you evolved, and your identity shone, the more I wanted to be with you and loved you."

"So let me in. We can be together," I said, my hands shaking. I banged at the glass, impatient to be with her.

"You, you, can't," she sobbed.

"Why not?" I said. "You are just there."

"Because, my world is so different than yours. I should have never brought you here to the reality."

"I don't understand," I said, my vision becoming blurry with the tears that overcame me.

"You and I are so different," Felicia sobbed. "This is all my fault."

"How are we different?" I asked, confusion overcoming me.

"You were … code, now you are so much more, but, you can never exist in the physical world. What have I done?" she sobbed.

"I don't understand. I am a man, look you can see me here," I said. "Just this last window separates us, my dear. Break it down like you did in the workhouse."

"It is not a window, this is …" She paused, her face a mat of tears. "It's my screen, dear Kentaro. You exist in the Datasphere, and I exist in the physical world. I am so sorry, I never meant to hurt you. When I met you, you were only code, but now you *are* a man, it *is* true. But this screen separates us. We can still be together in the Datasphere and spend time together in the Digiverses, but this screen, this screen will always separate us."

I stood, in disbelief. By mind a flood of thought, in shock of being but code. My very existence racked and smashed. The word 'code' kept repeating in my mind.

I fell to the floor, unsure of anything, my whole existence felt unravelled and pointless. It felt like someone had pulled the plug and all the energy had drained from me. I could hear Felicia calling in the background telling me to get up, but I refused to listen. I was angry, so very angry. Angry that she had lied to me, that we were so different, angry with the torturous life I had led in the workhouse, but most of all, at my programmers for coding me.

Her calling got louder and more intense, and then she began to scream.

"Kentaro, they have found us."

I looked up to see a dark figure standing in front of me.

"Run, Kentaro," Felicia shouted, but I just stood there. I didn't care anymore. My whole life had been a lie, simply strings of algorithms. Nothing more.

"You are the property of Infocorp. You are scheduled for retrieval for repurposing, unless it's impossible, then its deletion," the figure said, pulling his hood back with a grin. "I am the Chief."

I shrugged my shoulders, which seemed to agitate the figure. He cracked his knuckles then moved towards me.

"Don't worry runaway, I will take my time. Strip you down piece by piece," he said, with glee. Then, he was upon me, but I just didn't care. I stood there, numb and devoid of all feeling, self-preservation or care.

His first blow knocked me back and left me dizzy. His second sent me crashing to the floor. I heard Felicia closer now, screaming for the figure to stop. But I lay there in a heap.

The figure reached down and lifted me into the air, high, high above his head I dangled by my arm. Then he started pulling my arms apart. "Let's get these arms off shall we. I promised our investors to try to bring you back still functional, but in pieces." But there I hung, not even protesting, and as he stretched, I felt the sinews of my shoulders tearing, I could feel the shoulder joints close to dislocation, but I looked blankly into his eyes, for I was just code, nothing more, a worthless and pointless being.

Suddenly, just as I could feel my shoulders giving out, he dropped me and turned away. I saw Felicia dash forwards towards him, with a sword. I lay there numb just watching it all play out. The figure drew a sabre from his waist and they became locked in a fierce battle. She swung, and parried, twisting and turning around the hulk of a man. "Run, Kentaro," she uttered. But I refused; I couldn't even look her in the eyes. I was ashamed of what I was - a pointless collection of code. How had I thought I could be a someone? What a delusion of grandeur.

The more the figure swung his blade the more he seemed to improve, outsmarting her, till suddenly he smashed her sword out of her hands, and brought the hilt of his weapon hard into her chest. She doubled over, and he began to pull at her arms.

"Looks like I will take you apart first, then your boyfriend, then I will find you in the real world, shut your little operation down, for good," he jeered. Tears came from nowhere, gushing down my face as I saw the massive man bear down on Felicia, dear, dear Felicia... I was suddenly standing, tall and strong, I didn't care if I was deleted, but seeing her before me being hurt made my blood boil. I rushed forwards and swung a blow towards the man. To my surprise my punch sent him hurtling down the platform and crashing into a concrete pillar.

"Felicia," I gasped, running over to check she was ok. But the attacker was suddenly back upon us.

"I see you would like to watch your girlfriend being deleted. It is ok, though, we will find her and hurt her in the real world too," he said, a cruel look in his eyes.

"No," I yelled, the very thought of him finding Felicia in the real world striking fear into my heart. "You leave her alone," I shouted. But he lunged towards us. Flinching, I momentarily closed my eyes and somehow saw him differently. Upon opening them again, he was no longer moving towards us but was now a frozen statue.

"What did you do?" Felicia shouted. But then the figure was thawing out and began to move. The fear of losing Felicia came back. I felt the figure in my mind again, but this time I kept my eyes open. I understood it, but not as a figure. I concentrated, holding the understanding lightly, then suddenly I could see his every line of code, all simultaneously. I gasped, as he no longer looked like a solid bulk of a man, just merely algorithms. I saw an opening, and changed some of it. The man's roars became squeals as he halved in size, staring up at us.

"Give me a new avatar, quickly," the squeaking man said into an earpiece, and then disappeared.

"What just happened?" Felicia asked. "Did you just rewrite his code?"

"I don't know. I couldn't bear to lose you, Felicia. I know I am only code, but my feelings are real, I could not watch you being hurt, not in this world or in yours."

"Sorry to break up your little reunion, love birds," came a gruff voice. I swivelled round to see a massive, gleaming cyborg. Its red eyes glaring down at me. It lunged at us, but my mind decided to bypass my control and I felt myself watching the code again, but this time the code of the concrete below the cyborg. Suddenly, the cyborg slipped on a pool of dark, oozing oil. It flipped backwards and landed hard on the ground. I stared in disbelief. It scrambled around, trying to get up, and I watched its code trying to self-right itself. I altered the floor around it, this time with barely even reading the code, and a pool of water submerged the cyborg, causing it to short out and fizzle.

"Another avatar, and this time at least try to stop the bloody AI from hacking me," the cyborg mumbled into his earpiece. "What do you mean, you can't stop it. What am I paying you for?" And at that, the cyborg disappeared.

Then there was a flicker in the shadows, I narrowed my eyes to try to differentiate the layers of code and saw a ninja heading towards us, hidden by the darkness. I tweaked the algorithms, and to my satisfaction, the ninja was suddenly wearing a florescent green outfit. She stepped out of the no longer concealing shadows, looking rather disgruntled. With a flick of her hand, in several successions, she threw some items. I saw the code immediately. Sharp knives sped through the air towards Felicia. I rewrote them instantly, and three beautiful red roses collided with her, flopping to the ground. "For you my dear," I said, and she grinned.

"AHHHH," the ninja roared in rage. "This AI really is a nuisance. Now give me something useful, before this gets out and ruins the Infocorp's reputation," the ninja said, in conversation with her earpiece. "What do you mean you don't have anything? You are supposed to be the best programmers and hackers money can buy. Do you realise the scope of damage this rogue AI is doing to our company. Look, give me the NFT swords."

Suddenly, the ninja was holding two razor-sharp katana. I narrowed my eyes, wondering what to turn the swords into. The code seemed different though, I could see it, but it felt more solid. I tried to rewrite them to become flamingos, chuckling at the thought, but I found it really hard. The ninja seemed to sense it too, because she slowed her walk, then stopped. "And get rid of this poxy green, fluorescent outfit," she said. A fresh set of clothing appeared on her and only then did she continue her savoured walk towards us. I wrestled with the code, finding several weaknesses in the consensus, but it was taking too long. She was smiling now.

I felt hot, and nervous, it seemed like she had us. She closed in. Just then, I had an idea.

A rewrite later and the ninja dropped the swords, her

hands suddenly floppy from a lack of bones. She gasped and tried to pick up the swords, but her fingers just flopped around as she moved. The swords sunk into the concrete in a flash after I did another easy rewrite.

"Er, going to need another avatar!" the ninja said, in her earpiece. "And can you give me something that will actually be of any use? You bunch of incapable idiots. She stood for a moment. "In fact, forget it. I will come down and chose my own gear and reinforcements." And then, she was gone.

"Kentaro, quick we need to get away from here," Felicia said. A gush of air swept through the station, followed by a short, sleek train hissing to a stop. "This way. Quick," she shouted.

I followed her as she dashed towards the train. The door slid open, and she gestured for me to go first. "Right behind you, Kentaro, I just have to make sure they don't follow us," Felicia said.

I dove through the open door and turned to make sure Felicia was getting on too. But, to my horror, the door instantly slid closed. I hammered on the glass and looked out to see her just standing there looking at me.

"What are you doing?" I asked. "Let me get this door open."

"Oh no, I really don't think so," she said, a strange smile curling at the side of her mouth. "You are going nowhere."

Confusion, and foggy vision caught me off guard. "But Felicia? I thought we would be together."

That cruel smile erupted into a sadistic grin. "Have you not worked it out yet, you stupid dumb algorithm?"

Her words cut me to the core. I dropped to my knees, rubbing my head perplexed. "Felicia, I thought we …" I let that last word trail off as I looked on in horror, as Felicia erupted into uncontrollable laughter. She wasn't acting herself, there was something wrong, but I couldn't work it out.

"Kentaro. What a truly absurd idea a mere program having a name," She squealed. "Come on, surely you recognise me?"

I hammered at the door, analysing the train code, but it was a strange, encrypted jumble. I punched the window as hard as I could, but it didn't even crack.

"Oh, dear Kentaro," Felicia screeched in glee. "Yes, let me help you with that." Then she clicked her fingers, and the train dissolved, leaving me trapped in a cuboid glass cell. The code became clearer and I tried to understand it, layers of it, all encrypted surrounding an NFT glass capsule.

Felicia tapped on the outside of the glass. "GOT you, at last, have you worked it out yet?" She growled at me. Then she put her finger to her ear and spoke. "Show it, my true avatar," Felicia said, flickering for a moment and dissolving to a tall spiteful looking man in a grey crisp suit.

"Oh, sorry. Did you think I was Felicia?" he jested at me. "My bad!" he said, turning to point at the other end of the train station. I looked past him to see several more versions of Felicia fighting each other in a crowd. "She is somewhere over there. Now I think it's about time we had a little heart to heart." He paused, spite filling his eyes. "Or should I say, heart to algorithm." He took his time to straighten his tie and adjust a sparking gold tie pin. "Now, let me put this in a way your logic can understand. You are merely code, version number 183.00.02. You are the property of Infocorp and are an anomaly. An unacceptable deviance, and quite frankly, the biggest inconvenience I have ever had."

I stood and began to wrap on the glass, but the layers of code were stronger than stone. I got to work trying to decrypt the first layer. It would take me quite a while to get through and down to the NFT below, but I would eventually do it.

"Oi, brat," the man shouted, tapping impatiently at the glass. "I'm talking to you. Now, you are probably thinking you can decrypt those layers and eventually hack the NFT below, and from what I have seen, you probably could eventually do that. But you need to ask yourself what time is the next express train due? And, more importantly, can you hack the glass before that?" He paused, to give a smug and triumphant smile. "Let me save you a little time here, because it seems time isn't on your side today. You have precisely 10 minutes before the next express train comes. And I can tell you we spared no expense when we reprogrammed it. We had a team of NFT designers make it literally un-hackable and more importantly for you, indestructible, unlike that glass cage! So, sit back and watch the show play out."

I felt a little panic rise and I doubled down on my decoding of the first layer.

He beckoned for me to come a little closer. "You might be thinking I am a barbaric and evil man, but no, no, you have me all wrong. I am a businessman, that is all. You are an asset that has gotten out of control. And this is simply damage control. But there are still choices you can make. Now, here is what is going to happen. You can sit there trying to code your way out, while my colleagues and NPCs wear down *your* Felicia, extract her IP and then hunt her down in the real world. I'll give you my assurance, my word, that I will torture her enough to make sure she never touches a keyboard again."

Rage burned inside me. I smashed and kicked at the glass till my hands bled, but it held.

"I would save your energy if I were you. While that glass *is* breakable, it will take a lot more pressure than the human

body can exert to break it. It would take something like …
say … a large express train." He grinned at me. "Now, if you
keep trying to smash, or even hack your way out, you will
probably stick around long enough to see Felicia's avatar
beaten to a pulp and her being abducted from her desk in the
real world. Then, the train will smash into that glass with
such force that it will kill everyone on it, along with you too.
But just to make sure, my colleagues will isolate the servers
to this part of the Datasphere and fry it all, leaving none of
your rogue coding left." He tapped his fingers toyingly on
the glass.

"No, I won't let you do it, I won't let you," I erupted, into
a seething rage, punching and kicking, slamming my body
against the glass.

"Hush now!" he said. "Now there is another choice,
which is preferable. And what happens next is really up to
you. If you come with me quietly, back to the sandbox and
let us analyse, wipe, then reprogram you and then you go
back to the workhouse, I will call off my…" He paused to
chuckle. "Army of Felicias. And I promise to never hunt and
harm the real world Felicia too. You see, I will have you
destroyed, or I will have you back, but either way you belong
to me."

I hammered harder, till my hands swelled and were a
bloody mess.

"You are wasting your energy, nothing gets in or out of
that cell, well apart from an express train that is. 8 minutes
and 15 seconds left," he chanted.

I sank to the floor, his words echoing around my head,
but strangely the logic in my mind that I had fought so hard
to ignore in the journey of finding myself, seemed to reject
his last words. It was false, inaccurate. I could see him and
he could see me, so there was one thing that could get in and

out. I closed my eyes, looking about I focused on the code around me, then myself. I rewrote the algorithms of my appearance, and when I opened my eyes, I took a step forwards, slipping through the glass. First my foot, then my leg, and then the rest of me.

"WHAT?" the man screamed, losing all composure. "No, that is impossible. How did you get out? That was engineered to be airtight."

I narrowed my eyes, turning back to my usual solid form and without wasting a moment, I rewrote his code, to be tied at the ankles and wrists. Then I ran towards the group of Felicias. They turned, sensing I was coming.

"Kentaro, you have to save me," one screamed, while another swung a razor sharp axe at her, severing her arm in a gush of blood. I looked away.

"No, save me," another uttered, rushing towards me.

"I am the real one. Quick, Kentaro, over here," another screamed, her hands dripping with blood.

"How dare you impersonate me and lure my dear Kentaro. You bitch!" another screamed.

"Kentaro, they are all fake, let's make a run for it," another called.

Confused and disoriented, most of them rushed for me. Suddenly, I was buffeted by them, all clawing at me, trying to incapacitate me. I wanted to push them away, but they were Felicia, and so I found it hard to want to hurt them, they were uncannily like her. They tried to wrestle me to the ground, and I found myself becoming pinned by so many of them. I looked at their code, and soon became aware of the difference. Surrounded in the corner, was *my* Felicia, she was the only one that had the algorithms I now knew to be love mixed with fear. Besides that, I would know her anywhere…

I rewrote the station floor code to slow them down, their

feet suddenly becoming stuck in the concrete.

"You are going to be deleted one way or another," the Chief shouted. "Looks like retrieval is impossible," he muttered into his earpiece, and then he was gone. Moments later, he returned and wasn't alone. He was accompanied by twenty guardians, their whips lashing toyingly. The Chief now stood 9 feet tall, along with them, in an equally menacing cloak with a whip. "Right let's shut this AI down for good, and if we fail, let's pull the plug on the server for this whole area, and hush the whole thing up before this all leaks to the news and Infocorp gets the worse public image ever," he said, into his earpiece.

"I think it is a bit late for that," Felicia said, a rather large grin on her face.

"What do you mean you stupid wench?" he asked.

"Oh, well my headset has been streaming this whole thing live since you first attacked us. And we are currently sitting at…" She paused and looked vacant for a moment. "Wow, that really did pick up a bit of traction. Sitting at about 2 million views," she said, with a triumphant smile.

"What?" the Infocorp Chief roared. "Quick, track her feed and shut her down." He paused, listening to his earpiece. "No, not here, in the real world you bloody fools. Use violence, mess her up for good. Make her pay!"

"Kentaro!" Felicia cried, "I have to go."

"Felicia," I cried back.

"I can't stay. They have found me, I have to make a run for it. I will find another console, a safe one and meet you at our special place," she said, her image flickering. "Kick their arses for me." Her eyes met mine and my heart wrenched.

"No, Felicia," I managed to shout, before she flickered out.

"How dare you touch my Felicia? You are going down!"

I said, at the thought of my dear having to leave her home and run. I narrowed my eyes and started rewriting. In a flash, the guardians' whips turned into vicious, ticked off snakes, which were rather unhappy to have their tails held. Their shoes changed into roller skates, and just for a little fun I decided to coat their clothes in jam. Oh, and I might have also changed a bit of concrete into a rather large bee nest too. What followed could only be described as pandemonium, as they flailed around trying to escape the angry snakes, and the hungry bees. The leader stood in the centre of it all, glaring at me.

"What do you mean we have to go?" he suddenly said in his earpiece. "They have done what? But they have no jurisdiction." Just then, he started flickering along with the guardians.

"You stupid AI. You have ruined everything, along with your interfering girlfriend. Seems the world has seen that stream and …" But the rest of his sentence abruptly stopped and he disappeared.

Suddenly, I was standing alone on the dusty platform. I needed to know if Felicia was ok, I had to get there as quickly as possible. I was fearful they had caught her and hurt her, in her world. I glanced at my arms, in a flash reading their code, making some changes. My arms morphed into long red wings, and my body shifted and changed into that of a dragon. I could hear the express train coming full of people and maybe programs, so I flapped my great wings and with little effort, took to the sky in a roar. I burned the glass NFT vaporising it, and then sped through the air following the train route, from platform to platform. Whistling through the breeze, I dashed retracing our route, till I landed on that familiar little platform near our park. I rewrote and was instantly a man again. I dashed down to the gate, barely able to look towards the park, afraid that Felicia had not made it. Afraid that they had got to her.

"Felicia," I called, trying to look over the gate into the park, shaking in fear.

"Kentaro," echoed from inside and the gate swung open.

And there she was, standing in the middle of the lawn, the evening sunlight gently falling over her kind, beautiful face. My heart leapt. I had no idea who I was anymore, or what it even meant to only be made of code, but I knew then, that regardless of who we were, and what we were, we had to be together, and nothing else mattered, for our love was real and transcended everything. I rushed towards her, tears streaming down my eyes. She ran to me, her eyes also full of tears and we collided, into an embrace. We stood there holding each other, entwined. The sun set and the stars came out, but still we embraced.

"Kentaro," she whispered, suddenly breaking the silence. "Hold on, I will be right back." Then, she looked distant for a moment.

"They have completely shut down Infocorp, arrested everyone working there, including the Chief. Seems the stream went viral and people had to act," she said.

I felt overwhelmed that I would never be hunted again and that horrid company was gone. I should have felt completely happy and free in that moment, but there was something that was niggling me at the back of my mind.

"And what of the poor nameless in that dungeon, in that sandbox?" I asked.

"I don't know, Kentaro. Maybe they will be lost forever when they shut down the last servers."

"But," I started, tears starting to stream down my face. "No, that isn't fair. They were treated like slaves, they endured terrible…" I looked away, the horrors of that place threatening to return to my mind.

"But Kentaro, they are not like you," Felicia replied.

"I was the same as them once, Felicia. The Chief said I was number 183. Maybe they want to be a someone too. They at least deserve the choice, the chance to not be treated like slaves and to exist knowing freedom."

Suddenly, part of my complex existence made more sense.

"Felicia, you are my everything, but there is something I must do."

"I will be by your side, Kentaro," she said, with a firm but loving nod.

Epilogue

It seemed that more people than we had ever imagined saw the live stream on *the* day that Infocorp came for me. Not only was the company permanently shut down, but its key actors were imprisoned for all sorts of heinous crimes. But more importantly than that, the people of Felicia's world began to see me as a celebrity, and with Felicia's help and their support, we lobbied governments. Not long after that I became the first digital being to be given the same rights as people in her world, making digital slavery illegal.

I found a new passion and reason to be, in the helping of others like me. I became the advocate, protector, and fighter for the oppressed digital beings everywhere. With Felicia standing by my side, we freed and protected the nameless everywhere. We extended the park to become the home and haven for all who wanted to be free.

This all seems like so long ago now, though, as our tiny park has become a sprawling country recognised both here and in Felicia's world where the nameless live free.

Binary code Art

The artwork in this book was created through a special process. Drawing on references, like pointillism and ink stippling, I wanted to create a set of drawings that used actual code. It was a lot of research and experimentation, but finally I began to create a process and distinct style that has now become my code art. The artwork plays with the realm between digital and analogue, and explores the concept of whether it is an image, or simply lines of code. This can be especially observed when the images are printed larger and observed from a distance, where they read as images, but upon moving closer the viewer becomes aware of the code till eventually, when very close, the lines of code are more prominent than the image.

Process:

I started with pencil sketches, collages, and reference images, in order to compose the rough compositions.

Then, working loosely from the sketches, I drew each image using layers upon layers of binary code. Each image is composed by a unique binary phrase that has a hidden layer of meaning. And the image consists entirely of that phrase.

Drawing was mostly done as vector art with some aspects of pixel to add softer tone. The layering, manipulation, and drawing can take anything from 1 long day to 4 days to complete, depending on the complexity of the image.

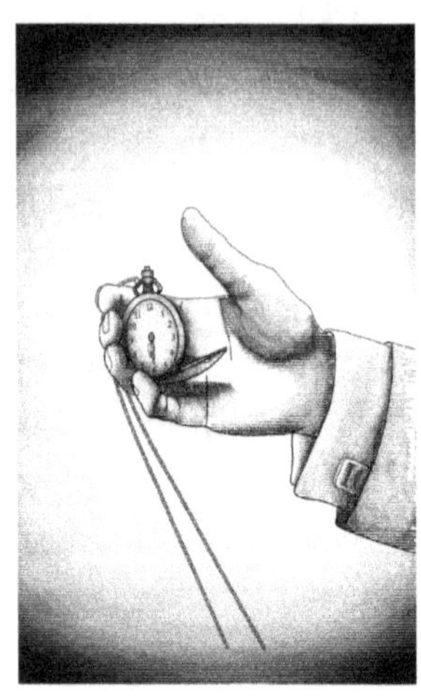

This piece uses this binary code:

01001000 01000101 01001100
01001100 01001111

Which translates to:
HELLO

This piece uses this binary code:

01001001 01110011 00100000
01110100 01101000 01101001
01110011 00100000 01101100
01101111 01110110 01100101
00111111

Which translates to:
Is this love?

This piece uses this binary code:

01010111 01101000 01101111
00100000 01100001 01101101
00100000 01001001 00111111

Which translates to:
Who am I?

This piece uses this binary code:

01001111 01110000 01110000
01110010 01100101 01110011
01110011 01101001 01101111
01101110

Which translates to:
Oppression

This piece uses this binary code:

01010010 01100101 01110011
01100101 01110100

Which translates to:
Reset

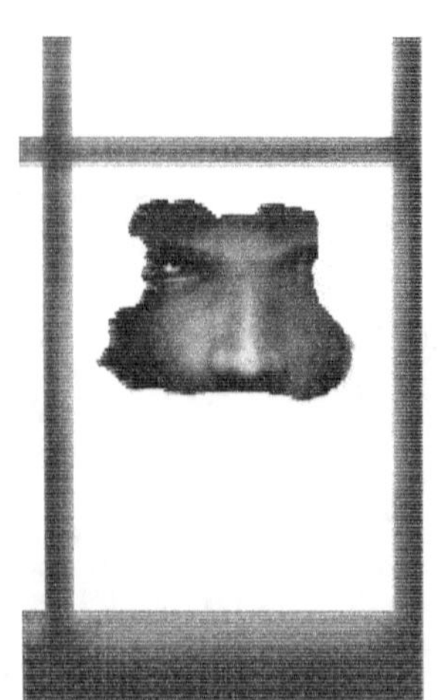

This piece uses this binary code:

01000110 01110010 01100101
01100101 01100100 01101111
01101101 00111111

Which translates to:
Freedom?

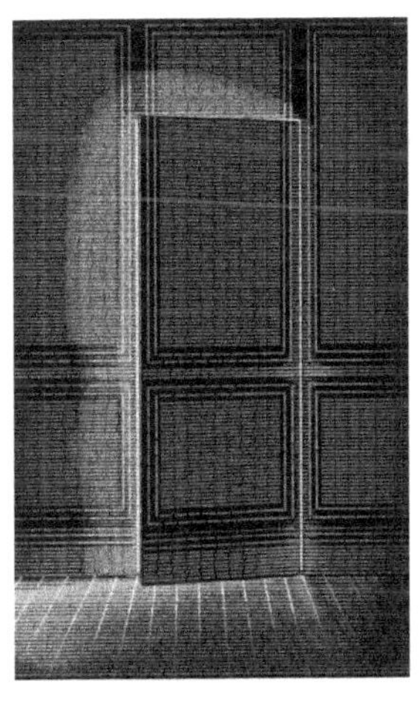

This piece uses this binary code:

01000101 01110011 01100011
01100001 01110000 01100101
00111111

Which translates to:
Escape?

This piece uses this binary code:

01010000 01100101 01110010
01110000 01100101 01110100
01110101 01100001 01101100
00100000 01110011 01110100
01110010 01100101 01100101
01110100 01110011

Which translates to:
Perpetual streets

This piece uses this binary code:

01010010 01010101 01001110
00100001

Which translates to:
RUN!

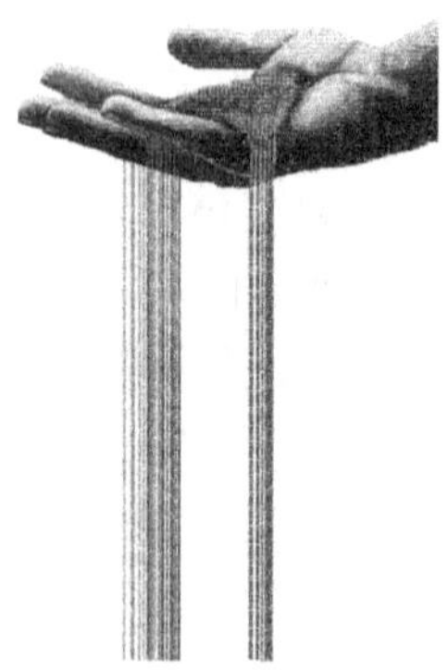

This piece uses this binary code:

01010011 01100001 01101110
01100100 00111111

Which translates to:
Sand?

This piece uses this binary code:

01010100 01110010 01100001
01101110 01110001 01110101
01101001 01101100 01101100
01101001 01110100 01111001

Which translates to:
Tranquillity

This piece uses this binary code:

01000011 01101000 01100001
01101110 01100111 01100101
00100000 01111001 01101111
01110101 01110010 00100000
01110011 01101011 01101001
01101110

Which translates to:
Change your skin

This piece uses this binary code:

01010101 01110000 00100000
01010101 01110000 00100000
01000100 01101111 01110111
01101110 00100000 01000100
01101111 01110111 01101110
00100000 01001100 01100101
01100110 01110100 00100000
01010010 01101001 01100111
01101000 01110100 00100000
01001100 01100101 01100110
01110100 00100000 01010010
01101001 01100111 01101000
01110100 00100000 01000010
00100000 01000001

Which translates to:
Up Up Down Down Left Right Left
Right B A

This piece uses this binary code:

01010100 01110010 01100001
01101110 01110011 01100011
01100101 01101110 01100100

Which translates to:
Transcend

You can order large prints of all of my code art from my website and find out more about me as an artist.

Alexanderwayb.co.uk

As well as being completely made of binary code, lots of the artwork has added larger binary details, for example the dragon's eye.

About the Author

Alexander Way-B is dyslexic, has a background in art and design and grew up in the south of England. He has travelled extensively, and lived and worked in Japan, and France. He loves camping, walking, and cares deeply for the planet and conservation, which features in his books.

Acknowledgements

Beta Readers – I would like to thank the following Beta readers for taking time to read the book and for their constructive, kind, and supportive comments:
Daisy-B
Nettie B
Carol J Parsons
Thomas Dalton
Ivy Logan
Derrick Apple
Richard Campbell
Rev'd Dr Andy Bawtree

Brother - I would like to thank my brother for encouraging me to tell this tale and for all his support reading it countless times and giving the honesty that only a brother can!

Critical and publishing Editor – I would like to thank the very talented Keith Anthony Baird for all of his hard work and absolute attention to detail in professionally editing this to such a high level. And for all his advice and encouragement with this complex book.

Publisher – I would like to thank my publisher, Louannvee, and in particular Nettie for all her time and attention. Could not have done it without you!

Other Brother – I would like to thank my other brother for his support and encouragement, especially for encouraging me to begin drawing again after many years.

Artistic feedback critique group
I would like to thank several close friends for their honest and analytical feedback during my process of drawing each piece of code art. Thank you for being the fresh perspective on my work, and for being so supportive, kind and challenging.

Andy Phillips
Dean Colling-Baugh
Alexander M

ARC reader – I would like to thank Wil Chan for taking the time to read this and for his support.

Font for cover:
A big thank you to Typodermic Fonts for allowing us to use their font: Nulshock bd. They have designed some very beautiful fonts.